Season in the Sun:

The Saxon Witch Horror

Simon G Gosden

Any resemblance to real persons, living or dead, is purely coincidental.

The Year of our Lord 895 A.D.

The Viking raids in the south of England are intensifying, their reign of terror spreading throughout the land. Northumbria is entirely Viking and they are using the ports there to mount raids across the whole of Anglo-Saxon England. Wortinge, lies on the South Coast of Wessex, a small Saxon settlement of mackerel fishermen and farmers, at least it was . . .

Chapter One: And so it Begins . . .

The Viking longship arrived, concealed by the early morning October mist, came in quietly, ever so quietly, oars muffled and the crew ready and eager for the fight. The steersman guided them towards the narrow shingle beach and gently, their boat ground against the pebbled shore. The waves lapped almost silently around the hull, the seaweed swaying to and fro with every swash and backwash of the waves. Their leader, a bear of a man over six feet tall wrapped in furs, leather leggings and the distinctive Viking horned helm on his head leapt from the dragon prow and landed with a splash in a couple of inches of gently lapping water. His nose broken and his face scarred from years of conflict he looked terrifying. His fearsome eyes were distinctive, one brown and the other green. He was the legendary Viking leader, Ivar the Boneless, skipper of the longboat known as the Serpent of the North, his crew battle hardened veterans of hundreds of similar incursions. Instinctively he reached down to feel the shingle in his hands as the first of the villagers rushed towards him. The Viking simply flung the handful of pebbles in the man's face, and swung his light battle axe as though swatting a fly. He severed the poor man's head and lifting it up as grisly trophy he roared a terrifying challenge. Holding the head up before him in one hand; his axe in the other and joined by the rest of the crew that leapt from the longboat they charged up the beach as one, a tide of death making its irresistible way towards the village.

Then one of the Viking raiders screamed in pain as a villager already skewered on the blade of his sword managed to pull his way up the blade and proceeded to bite a huge chunk from the man's face. He fell to the ground writhing in pain as the man bit more chunks from his face; soon other Vikings began to fall under the relentless and fearless assault of these fearsome villagers. Viking blood soaked into the pebbles of the shore as more and more of the Northeners fell. Each body quickly surrounded by villagers feeding on the living flesh, tearing and ripping it from the body in bloody chunks and devouring it with horrifying ease and obvious delight.

"Odin's blood, this is sorcery," Leif yelled to his fellow oarsman Sven, as he tried to fend off two men and a woman who seemed intent on eating him too. "Bloody fucking witchcraft."

"Aim for the fucking head," panted Sven, "it worked for Ivar."

He lashed out at a couple of women snarling at him and baring their teeth. Then he slipped on the beach and went down beneath the howling mob. Within seconds the sound of screaming stopped as they started their gory feast. Leif swung his axe and both his female attackers fell as their heads spiralled away; crimson blood spattering across the beach and his face and chest. The woman seized her chance and sprung at him but he was quicker and caught her full in the chest with his sword and yet impossibly she began slowly but surely to move towards Leif, pulling herself towards him as the blade vanished into her chest, eyes blazing with as deep a hatred and a hunger as he'd ever seen. Fumbling at his belt he found his knife and plunged it into her eye, it went straight in to the hilt and she too fell to the ground in a lifeless mess. Leif pulled the knife out and wiped it on his leather trews; panting with exertion he took a moment to look around.

All around small groups of villagers were feeding on the good men of the Serpent of the Sea. Ivar still stood, dazed and in shock at this bloody reversal. Olaf counted about twenty of the original crew standing stock still like Leif and looking on in shock and astonishment at the sight before them.

Slowly, cautiously with swords and axes drawn they pounced on the feeding mobs, hacking them with their swords and when all were still they backed down the beach, towards the water and the relative safety of their longboat. Muscles straining, they worked together and pushed the Serpent back into the sea and when she was fully afloat they scrambled up the ropes and back on board.

On Highdowne Hill overlooking the scene of terrible carnage and violence an old wrinkled crone dressed in grubby rags cackled and danced a jig of delight whilst her male companion seated on a Saxon pony looked on with disgust and horror at the bloodbath barely a mile away.

"I told 'e it would work, I told 'e," she giggled insanely. "Mama knows best. Mama always knows best, tee he, tee he, tee he. With my potion you can destroy your enemies, tee he, tee he, tee he."

Athelstan turned to her and shivered with distaste, the old woman had been planning this for ages and when The Serpent of the North was seen from the cliffs further along the coast she arranged a banquet for the people of the village. Little did they know that their pork broth contained something so potent and terrible? Athelstan's men, about twenty well_armed bodyguards, had been told to avoid the foul brew and leave soon after. They saddled up and rode the short distance up the hill to await the Viking invaders.

"It's no way to wage war Mother," he snarled his disgust. "Witchcraft it is and I'll be damned if I'll use witchcraft against anyone, even those barbarians." He glanced over his shoulder at his men and nodded at the old crone.

"Seize her," he cried, "and let God judge her blasphemy."

At this the old crone tried to run away but within seconds two burly house-men had grabbed her and tied her arms behind her back and spitting and cursing she was dragged away.

Ivar stood at the bow as they swept back out to sea, looking landwards, hand on the giant serpent's neck and shook his head in disbelief.

"What the fuck just happened, what the fuck was that? Odin's blood," he screamed to no one in particular, and then turning in anger he called to Leif.

"Leif, how many men have we lost? How many injured?"

Leif looked about him, men covered in blood and gore littered the deck, and did a quick count. A dozen men looked unharmed and exhausted but at least eight men lay groaning or unconscious with nasty bite wounds.

"I reckon about a dozen who could use an oar," Leif shouted back to Ivar. "We can still get back home though."

Suddenly one of the injured went into a violent spasm and then started biting the man who was tending him. The scream echoed around the deck of the longboat and within seconds it was followed by others.

"Shit," screamed Ivar. "Kill them, kill them all!"

The unarmed and exhausted men stirred themselves but they were lethargic and battle weary and the shock and surprise caught them unawares. Ivar and Leif fought back to back but they were being pressed on all sides. Teeth ripped flesh, sword and axe hit bone. Ivar went down on one knee as one of the undead leapt on his back sinking its teeth into the nape of his neck. Leif was panting with the exertion but then he caught the sight of the squall out of the corner of his eye.

The squall hit the longboat with a blast of rain and a huge gust of wind. The creatures lurched to the side and as the first wave hit, the boat keeled over, the weight of the creatures added to the listing and the Serpent of the Sea started shipping water. Leif toppled towards the side trying desperately to keep on his feet but then the second wave hit it and the last thing Leif felt as the boat turned turtle was the teeth ripping his throat out. He looked up through a cloud of his own blood and saw the vast bulk of the longboat settling on top of him as he sank towards the muddy bottom of the English Channel . . .

Eventually after hours of her cursing and spitting and screaming they dragged the old crone down to the coast and hung her from a stunted oak just inland from the eerily deserted village. As she swung in the stiff sea breeze she screamed curses and pledged that her children would once again roam the shore to avenge her death. After she'd died they left her there a few days while the king's men roamed the shore on horseback looking for any of the abominations that had survived the shipwreck. After ensuring the villagers were well and truly dead they burned their bodies on a huge pyre made of driftwood and timbers from their abandoned hovels. When that was done they cut down the old hag and buried her as deep as they could to make sure that whatever sorcery she carried remained in her damned pit. Athelstan and his men left the following day and not a word was ever spoken about the sorcery on the South Coast.

Chapter 2: The Summer of 1974

It stirred, it was aware that the other had left, squeezing out through the hard packed sand, but it had no concept of time, or when it had left. It was alone, but it hungered . . . it hungered for flesh, it hungered for blood, it hungered for brains, but most of all it hungered for revenge. It lay in the cold wooden tomb in the damp and the dark, alone and angry . . . it roared once with hunger and loneliness and then slowly it went back into its latent state and waited. Its time was coming, it wanted revenge . . . it would not be long . . . it would be soon . . . and it would get its revenge.

Sean Jacobson was happiest at sea in the small 14ft Dory he called Naomi. The moon was out and the panoply of stars that revolved above him was awesome on this balmy summer night. He was about a mile offshore checking his crab pots and the seine net he'd deployed the night before. The sound of the light swell lapping against his clinker built Dory was as comforting to him as ever, sometimes he'd simply lie back and fall asleep in the tranquillity of it all. On nights like this he imagined he was the last man on Earth, something that he found a strangely pleasant idea. The crab pots were a waste of time but as soon as he started to pull in the seine net he knew he had something on. It felt as heavy as the night he'd caught a hundredweight of thornbacks. He'd made a good few quid selling them to the restaurants in Worthing as skate wings. Sean was a Normandy landing veteran, he'd come back from the war traumatised, shell shocked and the fishing was just right for him as he didn't have to socialise with too many people, he preferred it that way. Naomi was his ex-wife, she left him when his drinking got too bad in the early 60s and now his boat was the only reminder he had of her. She was a sturdy craft, broad across the beam, stable and safe . . . he smiled at the thought that she was just like Naomi too. He saw something in the net, it looked a little lifeless but then it stirred, he reached over to pull it aboard when a white skeletal hand grabbed his arm. He lurched backwards inadvertently dragging the creature over the gunwale, he sensed the malevolence and hatred in those dark dead eyes. Its flesh was rotten, the vile stench of the putrescent flesh made him gag, it towered over him, almost impossibly tall. Fragments of leather clothing fell from the creature, but it was those eyes that he kept looking at.

"Shark eyes," he thought to himself. "But different fucking colours." Staggering back his feet got tangled up in a crab pot and he fell backwards cracking his head on the metal fuel tank that lay beside the outboard. He was probably dead before the creature got him. It ripped his throat out, revelling in the shower of blood and then started feasting on the rest of the body. Fully sated it slithered over and dropped back over the side leaving the corpse of poor Sean at peace at last floating in the gentle arms of Naomi . . . where he'd always wanted to be.

"Midnight at the oasis, send your camel to bed." I woke up on Sunday morning with that tune going over and over in my head, I'd been around at Rick's last night and he'd bought the single from the local record shop in the morning. We always went down town every Saturday to look at the charts and listen to the records in the booths. We'd hung around there for an hour or so, hoping to catch the eyes of some of the girls we knew and then got on our bikes to cycle back home.

Home for me was a big old dilapidated house about a hundred yards from the beach in Goring just on the outskirts of Worthing. On a really stormy night you could lie in bed and hear those big beefy breakers crashing on the pebbled shore, you could smell the sea and hear the screeching cries of the gulls as they wheeled through the air, sometimes the wind buffeted the windows of my little bedroom and you could imagine the awesome power of the sea not very far away.

It was a couple of miles to the town centre and I looked forward to going down there every

Saturday during term time but school had finished on Friday and the whole of the summer stretched before me. A summer of fishing, a summer of music and if all worked out, a summer of girls.

I should introduce myself, the name's Sam, Sam Herbert, Sherbert to my friends and I am fifteen years old. I go to the local secondary school, just done my O Levels and next term it's A Levels. I probably will be taking History, Mr Wetherby's my History teacher and he's brilliant, Geography and probably Economics, but the Geology teacher's new and she's well fit, so I might change my mind about that. I've got a good group of friends. I am not that sporty, but I do play cricket and hockey for the school but I am not that geeky either, an inbetweener I suppose. I like *Doctor Who*, *Star Trek*, *The Twilight Zone* and I read Gollancz SF yellow jackets and the works of H. P. Lovecraft and Clark Ashton Smith as often as Goring library gets them in. I've got black curly hair, I am about five feet ten inches tall and I am fairly skinny even though, as my Mum says, 'I eat like a horse'. Mum's a nurse and Dad works in London, he catches the train from Goring Station to Victoria at some unearthly hour every day and gets back late grumbling about leaves on the line or signal failures and then gets up the next day at goddamn o'clock and does it all again. I am not going to do that; I haven't decided what to do but commuting to London is not going to be my career choice.

Sunday morning wasn't a lie in for me, it was the big paper round delivery of the week and with Maria Muldaur still reverberating through my head I got up washed and brushed my teeth, dressed in my usual flared Levi's, T-shirt, converse pumps and got the old three gear, green Raleigh bike out of the shed and set off. Green's Newsagents was a short cycle ride away. I loved this time of the day, no-one around just me on my bike and the gulls and the sounds of the sea. I got there and opened the door, the tinkling bell caused Mr Green to turn and smile. Mr Green's a short tubby man, very red faced with wispy grey hair, he always dresses in a white coat. Mum says he's a drinker but I've never seen him drinking, and he's up bloody early every day.

"Hello Sam," he grinned. "Just finishing up the papers, put the naffing kettle on and make us a brew." He nodded to the back room where the gas stove was. I brushed through the plastic fly screen and filled the kettle from the rusty tap; I lit the gas hob with a match and settled down to wait for it to boil. It didn't take long and with two mugs of steaming tea and went back into the shop and handed Mr Green his brew. He took a long swig and gasped with enthusiasm.

"You can't beat a bloody good cuppa," he smiled. "Your bloody papers are nearly ready. What do you think of that?" he nodded to the *Worthing Gazette* on the counter. I carried my tea over and gazed down at the headline.

FISHING BOAT FOUND ADRIFT – NO SIGN
OF THE OWNER
Fifth One this Month

"That's a bit worrying," I said. I'd already
resolved not to say anything about this to my dad
otherwise I could foresee a blanket ban on boat
fishing for the whole summer. What a disaster
that would be. I read more of the article and saw
the picture of a pensive and worried DCI Penrose
who was in charge of the investigation. There was
a number to call if anyone had any information.

"I wonder what's causing it?" I said to no one in
particular. "Was he drunk?"

"It'll be those bloody Russian submarines," Mr
Green hissed in anger, he hated the Russians,
probably just a teeny bit more than he hated the
bloody Chinks and the bloody Frogs and the
naffing Jerries . . . I smiled and collected the
bulging sack of papers and carried them out and
managed to get them on the cycle rack on the
bike and set off on my deliveries.

The papers were full of the demonstrations by
the National Front and the counter
demonstrations by those opposed to them in
which a student got killed. The pictures on the
front pages were pretty grim. The lad was only
twenty-one, I wanted to be at University when I
was twenty-one and going out on demos against
fascists, just like him.

The round took about an hour. I got home and put the bike in the shed; I went in the back door and the smell of frying bacon and fried bread assailed my nostrils; Mum was hard at work preparing breakfast.

"Wash your hands," she said. "There are cornflakes on the table and bacon and eggs will be about five minutes."

Without waiting I did as I was bid and was tucking into cornflakes before you could say Jack Robinson. Dad was sitting at the head of the table with his head stuck in the *Sunday Telegraph*.

He grunted to me and carried on reading, as I finished the flakes a lovely plate of cooked food was put in front of me, I smeared Marmite on the fried bread and tucked in with gusto. Mum looked on with mild distaste; she was never a big eater and hated Marmite about as much as I loved it.

"What you up to today?" she asked. "Going out in the boat fishing?"

"No not today, we've got to strip down that outboard and give it a thorough service, we don't want it going wrong during the summer. Change the spark plugs, clean the filters and make sure she runs smooth."

Dad grunted again.

"Bloody Harold Wilson," he said. "Man's a total disaster . . . you think what we all went through during the war and a bloody Labour Government to show for it. Harrumph. . . ." He cleared his throat noisily. Dad never failed to mention the war and how his generation had given everything for us to throw it all away.

"Charles," Mum snapped, "please no swearing at the table." I smiled to myself, I'd heard plenty worse than that at school and Mr Green was a consummate and proficient swearer. Sometimes I was surprised that he could get so many swear words into a single sentence.

"Just make sure you're back for afternoon tea." Dad glared at me from above the newspaper. Afternoon tea, God how I hated that but it was a ritual and Dad was a stickler for ritual.

"Sure Dad," I smiled. "What time would that be?" I asked demurely.

"Don't get smart with me lad, and can't you get your bloody haircut." His eyes narrowed menacingly.

"Charles. . . !" Mum glared at him.

"May I leave the table now," I implored. Mum nodded and as I left the room I heard her say: "Charles, what is the matter with you now. . . ."

I skedaddled fast before Dad started on one of his many rants about long haired hippies or left wing loonies or people on council estates. I was on my way to Rick's, Rick Grimes, he lived about thirty yards nearer to the sea than me and his garage was where we met most days after school and at weekends. He lived on his own with his mum, his parents got divorced when he was little and he had far more freedom than most of us. His mum even let him smoke in the garage!

"This Town Ain't Big Enough for the Both of Us" was blasting out from a tinny transistor radio as I approached the double garage doors. I opened them and saw Rick tall and skinny with his long hair in his loon pants and tie-dyed T-shirt working on the outboard. The garage was littered with fishing gear and tackle, in the middle of the floor was an old camping table and a handful of rickety deckchairs around it with an old Calor Gas light in the middle. Rick's hands were filthy with oil and we nodded to each other as we acknowledged the work we had to do. The outboard was mounted on a hand made rig we'd put together with some off cuts and driftwood. If we needed to test it, we had an oil drum in the corner full of water that we could drop the outboard in still on the rig and fire it up. Rick had the spark plug out and was testing the gap with a feeler gauge so I set to removing the carburettor so I could get to the filter.

Rick and I had known each other since forever, Nursery School, Primary School and Secondary School, we just got on and sometimes we could go for hours without saying much at all, especially when we were fishing.

"The *Gazette* says a fisherman's gone missing," I said by way of conversation. "That's the fifth one this year. Mr Green says it's the bloody Russians!"

"Bloody hell, I wonder who it was this time?" Rick exclaimed. We knew a good many of the fisherman who still plied their trade off Worthing and Goring beach. It was a tough life, hauling your boats over the shingle daily and catching the tide at all times of the day and night. The profits were slim and the work back breaking. It wasn't what we wanted we were purely fishermen for fun.

"I don't know, maybe we could have a cycle along the sea front later and ask a few questions?"

Rick nodded approvingly and turned back to his work. After fifteen minutes or so the door creaked open and Glen Green came in whistling "Sugar Baby Love" and boy could he whistle. GG is the son of Mr Green the newsagent, that's how he gets to see all the cool American comics. GG is a bit tubby, blond hair and blue eyes, more than a touch of acne though but he sure can hold a tune. Rick played the guitar and when the two of them got together the results could be pretty spectacular. Me? I was tone deaf and got kicked out of the school choir for ruining the Christmas Carol Concert, but that's another story.

"Rick, Sherbert," he smiled. "How's it hanging?" GG loved *Happy Days* and would often slip into what he considered to be cool American slang. I just prayed he never tried it in front of my dad!

"Yea, we're pretty good," I responded. "Just getting this little beauty ready for a summer full of fun, fishing."

"And flirting?" GG asked.

"If we're lucky," Rick smiled. "If we're lucky."

"The tide's high at noon tomorrow," GG told us. "We can get up early, dig bait before breakfast and be out on the water by 10.30. The weather's going to be lovely then we can spend the rest of the afternoon on the beach chatting up the ladies!"

To be honest none of us were any good at that at all apart from Sean Barton. Sean was good looking lad, some said he looked a bit like Rod Stewart and he wore his hair in a Rod mullet, I never could see the resemblance myself. There was no doubt though he had the gift of the gab. He fancied himself something rotten and always dressed cool but the girls found him irresistible. It was strange that he wasn't here yet, but he was dead lazy and sometimes wouldn't get up till really late. His mum and dad were loaded and drank like fish, so I guess if they weren't getting up early Sean had no need to either. His dad had a fridge his garage which was always full of ice-cold Foster's lager and we'd pop around sometimes—just to check on the quality you understand . . .

"GG that's a great idea," I beamed. "Let's start as we mean to go on. I get the feeling that this summer is going be the best ever."

As I said that Sean walked through the door with Sasha Williams. The three of us looked at each other with astonishment; you could actually hear the sharp intake of breath. Sasha is the girl that everyone wants to go out with, carnival queen, the star of every school musical production we've ever done, and just drop-dead gorgeous with raven hair and dark brown eyes, a flawless lightly tanned complexion and legs that go on for ever. You could almost see Sean puff himself up with pride.

"Hi, losers," he smirked. "How's the service going? By the way do any of you know Sasha?"

We mumbled a host in inanities, tongue tied and shy—it must have been pitiful to watch. In the end we eventually all said hello and got back to work.

Sasha sat herself down on a deckchair, crossing those pretty long legs of hers and I clocked both Rick and Glen casting appreciative glances in her direction.

Rick explained to Sean about the proposed fishing trip, he smirked at us.

"My mum and dad are away for a few days; Sasha's staying over tonight . . . I don't think I'll be up early tomorrow," he winked at us.

We all looked at Sasha and she just smiled beautifully back. We were lost for words, a girl, staying over. That was unheard of and we were all insanely jealous. The outboard was done so we lifted her over to the oil drum and I pulled the cord to start her up. The engine erupted with a cough of blue smoke and then sent a huge plume of dirty water high into the air, crashing down on poor Sasha. She screamed and then ran from the garage with Sean trailing behind her pleading for her to stop.

I started laughing, so did GG and Rick and within seconds we were lying on the floor in utter hysterics. Sobbing and snorting with laughter we eventually got the place cleared up. Rick lit a fag and I cadged one off him. I wasn't a regular smoker but every now and then I enjoyed a puff or two. We stood with GG at the garage door looking down to the sea.

"It's a record spring tide tomorrow," said Rick. "The tide will go out further than it's ever done before and we three lads will be down there at 5am digging for lugworms."

"I think Sean may well be joining us," I giggled. "Splish, splash," and we all dissolved into laughter again.

Mrs Grimes came out with some tea and sandwiches and we sat on the front wall simply chatting about what the summer held for us. Towards the sea at the end of the road was the café and beyond it the sewer outfall about three quarters of a mile from the beach. You could just hear the waves on the beach and the sound of happy day trippers laughing and playing on the greensward. It was still and warm; a glorious Sunday evening, how I envied those families enjoying life together just sitting around a picnic blanket chatting to each other normally with some scotch eggs, pork pies, pickled onions and maybe a bottle of Corona or a flask of tea.

"Shit," I belloved. "It's tea-time." I stamped on my fag and bolted for home, the laughter of GG and Rick ringing in my ears.

DCI Tim Penrose looked down quizzically at the bloody mess in the boat. The coastguard had found the Dory drifting off Shoreham on Sunday morning and they'd towed it into the safety of the harbour around lunchtime. Penrose, as he liked to be known, had got the call and together with DC Lisa Griffin they'd responded with the flashing blue lights as they sped along the A27 from Brighton to Shoreham in their Triumph 2000. Penrose enjoyed driving the Triumph, it had a throaty roar to it and with its six cylinder 2.5 litre engine it could eat up the road. Lisa Griffin on the other hand always found driving with Penrose rather nerve-wracking as she spent most of the time putting her foot on her imaginary brake or holding on to her seat belt for dear life.

Penrose was thirty-nine years old, and he'd lived in and around Brighton and Hove for most of his life. He was a confirmed bachelor and though he'd dated on and off he'd never met the right girl yet. Lisa, on the other hand, was engaged to Matt Briggs, a rugby playing PC based in Brighton's main Police Station. They were planning to get married next year and both were saving like mad. Penrose, prematurely bald, six-foot-tall and powerfully athletic in build towered above Lisa who was a dainty, slender blonde. Many a Brighton drunk or ex-lag had mistaken her diminutive size as a weakness to their cost. She was a black belt in Judo and could fell anyone and immobilise them in seconds.

"Another one Lisa," Penrose sighed. "How many is that this year?" He knew the answer but he just wanted it confirmed.

"Five, Guv," said Lisa, "and we don't have a single clue as to what's going on . . . it's really bloody weird."

"Whose boat was it."

"An ex-army lad, fishing of Worthing Beach, according to the local foreshore records office. I spoke to them on the phone just now. Man by the name of Sean Jacobson who lives, er . . . sorry Guv, lived on his own in Goring just beyond Worthing. He fished for crabs and mackerel and bass in season. Had a little spot on the foreshore where he sold his catch direct to the public. According to the records office a quiet guy, kept himself to himself." Lisa shut up as Penrose stared at the boat bobbing in the water below blood stained and abandoned.

"Okay," he said emphatically. "Let the boffins have a good gander and tell them to report to me on Monday morning. I want to know as much as possible about what happened in that boat. In the meantime, you and I are off to Goring." He turned perfunctorily and marched off to the car. Lisa gave her instructions to a couple of PCs and followed her Guv back to the car. In seconds the car was roaring along the A27 over the Shoreham Bridge and headed for Goring.

I burst, panting with running, into the lounge not knowing what to expect. Dad was standing by the fireplace and the look he had in his eye was a not a good one.

"What time do you call this?" he snapped.

"Five o'clock," I nodded in the direction of the grandfather clock by the door. "At least that's what the big fella says." I heard Mum's sharp intake of breath.

"Don't get smart with me boy," he growled.

"Charles," Mum said. "You promised."

"Tea is at four-thirty, on the dot. Please ensure that you get here on time in future. I know you don't go to church on Sunday any more since the unfortunate incident, so there's no reason for you not to plan your day efficiently and be here on time."

I looked down at my shoes and smiled. The unfortunate incident involved Christmas Eve midnight mass and my grass snake, Lenin, finding its way into the vicar's vestments just prior to the service and how was I to know the vicar had an aversion to snakes? Anyway the service had to be terminated and the vicar sedated but not before he'd used some language that even Mr Green would have been proud of. I wasn't exactly banned from the Church after that but my presence wasn't required on a Sunday any more.

"You aren't laughing at me boy, are you?" Dad snarled.

"No way," I retorted. I was tempted to say daddy-o but the consequences wouldn't have been good for anyone.

"Anyway," Dad carried on, "your mother and I have been upstairs having a lie down."

I grimaced, "having a lie down" was a euphemism I was sure.

"And we both inadvertently dropped off for forty winks. So tea has only just been served. Your good luck Sam, your good luck."

Mum smiled and joined in. "Sam," she said, "we've some good news, it's hard to say this any other way but you are going to be a brother to a new baby."

"Bloody hell," I said and Dad moved towards me sharply raising his hand.

Mum though, moved quicker and blocked his advance.

"Stop, Charles, it's bound to be a shock to the boy. After all this time," she pleaded with him. He struggled internally and then turned away, smashing his fist down onto the fireplace in anger.

"Sam, have some food, please," she continued.

I took a plate from the coffee table and sat down with some fish paste and cucumber sandwiches and a cup of tea in a bone china mug. Mum had made fairy cakes that sat invitingly on a three tier cake stand. My mind was in a whirl though. A brother or sister, it was beyond my comprehension.

"Well," Dad snarled, his temper was well and truly up. "Cat got your tongue?'

"Congratulations," I stammered. "When is the baby due?"

"We think in January," Mum said, "but we'll know for sure later this month."

"Wow." That's not what I expected at all. I ate my sandwiches and tucked into some fairy cakes. I have to say they were delicious.

The rest of the afternoon and evening passed in a daze. I made an excuse around 8pm and made my way to my room. I set the alarm for 4.30 am—we were meeting at Rick's at 5 am with forks and buckets. We need enough bait for a good session, digging lugworms was backbreaking work, but you couldn't fish without bait . . . sleep didn't come easily to me that night as I thought about all the changes that a new baby would bring to this fairly dysfunctional household. I lay awake for a long time tossing and turning and then just before I fell asleep I swear I heard an awful anguished howl from far out at sea.

The Triumph pulled up with a satisfying screech outside Sean Jacobson's house, the radio blasting out "Summer Breeze" by The Isley

Brothers. It was late Sunday afternoon. Penrose and Lisa peered inquisitively at the little bungalow from the car. It looked well cared for, reasonably well decorated and the nets looked as though they'd been washed recently.

"No sign of life," Lisa said.

"Well, let's give it a go." Penrose opened his door and stretched his tall frame appreciatively.

They both made their way up the path through the neat front garden to the door. Penrose knocked loudly and after a few seconds without a sign of life he lifted the doormat, revealing a shiny Yale key. He picked it up and carefully opened the door. Cautiously they made their way into the house. Fish and chip wrappers and dirty plates littered the couch and the coffee table. A couple of empty bottles of beer sprawled on the floor and the sofa looked as if it had been slept on frequently. You could see into the kitchen and the sink was piled with dirty cups and plates, a bluebottle flew languidly around in its looping haphazard way.

Lisa pulled a face. "Not very house-proud is our Sean, is he?"

"I think he lives on his own," Penrose smiled.

"So do you," Lisa retorted, "but not like this. It looks completely different from the outside. This is a pig-sty."

"Appearances can be deceptive Lisa, never judge a book by its cover." Penrose grinned.

By the big TV on the sideboard there was a wedding picture and alongside it a picture of a man dressed in uniform. Sgt Sean Jacobson, Essex Regiment it stated simply.

"The Essex regiment were at Gold Beach on D-Day, June 6th 1944, they took heavy casualties."

"This is the same man." Lisa pointed to the wedding photo. "It's dated 1956, so he got through the war, came back, got married, got divorced and ended up dead in the bottom of a fourteen-foot Dory. Not much of a life."

"At least he had some life." Penrose looked rueful. "A lot of those poor lads' lives ended on D-Day, don't forget that."

Lisa nodded.

"Well, there's not much here for us," she said. "Fancy a pint?"

Penrose grinned and reached into his pocket. "Heads or tails?" He flipped the coin and nonchalantly caught it.

"Heads!" Lisa yelled.

"Heads it is." Penrose shook his head. The Henty then it was to be, a village pub in Ferring about two miles away. Carpets that actually held you up they were so sticky, a jukebox so loud it made your ears ache, the whole place stinking of tobacco smoke and other more exotic substances, but you could get a nice pint of mild and bitter there. He preferred the more salubrious surroundings of the Black Rabbit at Arundel, a lovely quiet country pub beneath Arundel Castle, lying alongside the River Arun. Gorgeous spot for a Sunday evening drink . . . then to his surprise Lisa said: "To the Black Rabbit then," and giggled at his confusion. "After the day we've had we need some thinking time."

Albert 'Bertie' Brooks was on his way back to shore. He'd set his crab pots and two seine nets and now all he wanted to do was to get back home, pop his waders off and snuggle into his slippers, tuck into a large glass of malt and watch TV. He looked at the luminous dial of his Timex wristwatch, a present from his dear old lady and reckoned that if he got back soon he'd catch the last ten minutes or so of *Sunday Night at the London Palladium*, he loved that show. Jim Dale made him crease up sometimes. The outboard roared away and he leant back at the stern arm over the tiller. The salt spray made him feel alive and the phosphorescence wake meandered behind him shining in the moonlight. He could see the streetlights behind the café and just make out the spire at the top of church lane in the distance. He had a compass but like most of the small fishermen he used line of sight navigation most days and nights. He could just make out the waves breaking on the pebble beach ahead of him when the outboard motor reared out of the sea. His arm smashed against the transom and the boat nearly turned turtle.

"Fucking hell, what was that?" Bertie shouted at no one in particular. He shut off the outboard and lifted it up, the cotter pin was smashed, the propeller spun uselessly.

"Shit, we must have hit something . . . but there's nothing out here at all!" He stood at the back of the boat and stared at the dark black water. All of a sudden the hairs on the back of his neck started to bristle and Bertie felt very, very alone, very scared and exposed out here on water a hundred yards at least from the shingle beach. To be honest he'd never felt so scared in all his life . . . He left the outboard where it was and grabbed at the oars and flinging them through the rollocks he started rowing frantically to shore. Breathlessly he jumped out of the boat and ran up the beach to the manual winch, he frantically pulled the boat up the shingle and then lay their panting and terrified.

He started crying and sobbing with fear when he heard an outlandish anguished howl from far out at sea. He needed a good drink and it might not just be the one either!

Paul Wetherby, history teacher and local historian, leant back in his deck chair and gazed over at his gorgeous wife Francoise. He'd met Francoise in Normandy as the British Forces worked their way through, liberating village after village and town after town. They'd fallen in love instantly and Paul had promised to come back after the war was over. He kept his promise and they got married in 1947 and Paul brought his new wife back to the village he grew up in and got a job teaching at the school he actually went to before the war. Francoise, who'd trained as teacher in France, eventually got a job at the same school and life settled down. Their cottage was a picture postcard cottage with climbing pink and red roses over the porch, two apple trees and a glorious vegetable patch which they both tended with love and care. Paul and Francoise felt as liberated as Sam had felt earlier that day and looked forward to six weeks' rest and relaxation. Francoise, dark haired, olive skinned and beautiful was a typical Normandy girl; she loved her food, her Gauloise and her Calvados. Paul, increasingly a Francophile, was besotted with her and together they cooked amazing meals with the vegetables they'd grown in their own plot. Tonight it had been Chicken a la Normande, chicken in calvados with apples and onions from the garden. They'd shared the washing up and now were chilling in the garden looking forward to an early night and a long lie in on the first morning of the summer break.

"That was a stunning meal," Paul said and raised his Café au lait in a mock toast to his wife.

Francoise acknowledged his toast with a blown kiss and smiled seductively at him.

"The best is yet to come," she murmured in an exaggerated and throaty French accent.

The mood was broken by an otherworldly anguished howl that came from far out at sea. Francoise's head jerked towards the sound . . . and Paul started up so fast that he spilt some of his coffee on his shirt.

"Mon dieu, what the hell was that?" You could hear the quiver of real fear in her voice.

"I have no idea," said Paul. "No idea at all but I do think it's time to go in. What do you think?"

Francoise nodded enthusiastically and they hurried inside. Paul locked the doors and then went around again to check they were all locked. When they got into bed their cuddles weren't amorous, as she had intimated, they were mutually supportive and they eventually fell asleep in each other's arms for comfort.

Penrose was at the bar at the Black Rabbit, it was getting late by now so he ordered a pint of Courage Director's Bitter, a glass of dry white wine for Lisa and a round of ham and pickle sandwiches. Having paid for the drinks he took them out to the table that Lisa had found for them on the small terrace garden that overlooked the river. It was an idyllic spot and as he sat down Penrose could hear the crickets chirruping in the undergrowth and he spotted a bat flying across the moonlit sky. The river glowed by the light of the moon and Penrose could just make out Orion's belt in the night sky. Couples chatted amiably with each other, the buzz of intimate conversation was very relaxing. He took a large quaff of his pint and sighed in appreciation and relaxed back in his chair.

"So we've got five bodies in five boats in a month and not one single bloody clue, where are we going with this Lisa? I've got the Chief Constable on my back demanding answers. He's terrified the press are going to get hold of this story and run with it as some demented lunatic serial killer on the loose." He paused as the barmaid brought over the sandwiches and laid them on the table. He nodded his thanks to her and picking up one of the sandwiches he tucked in.

"We just need one good lead, Guv." Lisa reassured him. "Then we'll find the answer I'm sure."

Penrose leaned towards her and spoke softly but quite forcefully.

"That's not the real issue, the thing is those first four bodies, well they weren't dead."

Lisa's eyes widened in shock, Penrose continued.

"You know the first one, Jay Blunt, well the story goes that down at the morgue well some young lad was clearing up at the end of the day when he heard a racket coming from cold storage drawer where the body was kept. He pulled it open and the thing that had been Jay Blunt made a grab for him. Luckily for him he managed to kick the drawer back shut and crushed the things head. Bits of bone and brains splattered all over the floor. It didn't move after that but they found the poor lad screaming and lying on the floor in a pool of his own piss. He has been off sick since then and he's had to sign the official secrets act to prevent it getting out in the public domain. Now the boys at the morgue do a little incision and sever the spinal cord, just in case. They didn't need to do that with our lad Sean as his head was all stove in when he fell over and whacked himself on the fuel can.

Lisa shivered and took a big gulp of her wine. "Bloody hell, that's horrible."

Without warning the crickets went silent, across the river terrace the conversation hushed, there was a long moment of complete and utter calm and then the night was rent with an anguished howl, the like of which Penrose had never heard before.

"My giddy aunt, what in heaven's name was that?" Lisa asked.

Penrose finished his pint in one swallow. "I've no bloody idea whatsoever but suddenly I've lost my appetite Lisa, come on let's make a move."

Rick Grimes slept heavily, snoring gently, above his bed a huge Jimmy Hendrix poster looked down upon him and his six-string guitar on its stand at the foot of the bed, he was dreaming about playing a gig in a smoky venue with the new band Queen that everyone was talking about, the place was heaving but one busty blonde had caught his eye and he was looking forward to the after show party. He didn't appear to hear that anguished howl but he whimpered in his sleep and shifted restlessly, eyelids flickering as he played air guitar.

GG's bedroom was covered in posters of movie monsters and his tallboy was littered with meticulously hand painted models of famous movie monsters like Frankenstein, the Wolf Man, the Mummy and Dracula, a glowing skeleton stood beside them. He was fast asleep too when the unearthly sound reverberated through Sussex. Just like Rick he whimpered softly, turned over in his sleep and then started sucking his thumb, something that he hadn't done since he was three years old.

Sean was awake, fuming with Sasha. She insisted on going home to get out of her wet things and then her mum started quizzing her about what exactly was going on. It didn't take long for her mum to work out that Sean and Sasha had a cunning plan and within seconds she was grounded and he was being shown the door in no uncertain manner. He heard the howl, it terrified him. Alone in the house he got up and checked every lock on every door and window, then he went back to his bedroom shut the door and put his pillows on top of his head and wished for sleep that didn't come for a long, long time.

Chapter 3: Monday morning

The alarm clock woke me at 5 am, so I switched on the tiny transistor radio and Noel Edmond's cheery voice came at me over the airwaves, he'd taken over from Tony Blackburn last year and I quite enjoyed his banter and the silly gags he played on people. He started playing 'There's a Ghost in my House' by R Dean Taylor, which for some reason made me shiver. I got dressed quietly and crept downstairs made myself a cup of tea and had a quick bowl of flakes before I picked up my welly boots, bait bucket and fork from the garden shed and made my way down the road. Rick was waiting for me sitting on the wall with yet another fag on the go and within seconds GG joined us, punching us playfully on the arms we wordlessly headed towards the beach.

The mist thickened as we approached the sea, it wasn't thick enough to be called fog but it was quite eerie in the half light. The café loomed before us and we crossed the greensward before noisily making our way down the pebble bank and onto the sand. On our right was the large wooden jetty, with the storm drain and its seemingly constant supply of water falling from it even after the driest of dry spells; coming from the myriad of drains in Goring. On Bonfire Night we'd fire air bomb batteries or rockets up it from here and you'd hear the detonations echoing all over the place. It was quiet here on the sandy beach, the mist absorbing what noise there was from the other side of the pebble beach.

"Where are we heading?" GG asked.

"The normal place," Rick responded. "We'll head out toward the sewage outfall and start digging on that sand bank we dug last time."

"Okay," I joined in. "Can't wait; I reckon we might get some ragworms out there too."

We normally just dug for the fat juicy lugworms but sometimes if you were lucky you might come across a ragworm. Whiter and far more active they wriggled around very alluringly on the hook and the local sea bass loved them.

We started trudging out further from the beach, out boots digging into the hard packed sand and marking our trail as we went.

"Bloody hell GG, what did you have for breakfast, a plate of baked beans? That stinks." Rick laughed.

"That's not me," GG retorted indignantly.

"No, that's not a fart," I grimaced, "but whatever it is it's absolutely foul."

We stopped walking and I held up my hand motioning for them to be quiet.

"Listen, what's that noise?"

Barely audible I could hear a very light buzzing. We moved slowly forwards, conscious of how exposed we were on the beach, in the mist.

"What's that?" Rick pointed to our left.

Just ahead of us we could see something lying on the sand. It appeared to be moving, undulating with an unnatural movement. I picked up a stone that was lying on the sand and lobbed it towards the thing. As the stone fell nearby, a thick black cloud rose up into the air and headed towards us. Terrified we backed up and then screamed in panic as a million sand flies bombarded us, rushing past us and onwards towards the storm drain into which they vanished into it in seconds. An unnatural quiet descended, our nerves were in tatters. We looked at each other and at that moment if one of us had run we all would have; nodding in encouragement we slowly crept forwards. The stench got worse and worse, I'd been down to the sewage outfall at low water and that was bad but this was truly indescribable. We got within ten feet I suppose and GG stopped. "Bloody hell," he whispered, "it's a bloody body. But what the hell's wrong with it?"

The thing's torso was skeletal in the extreme, but it seemed impossibly long; it didn't appear to be wearing very much by way of clothes, some raggedy trousers and some rotten sheepskin thing, the flesh was pallid and wan, long broken fingernails, but it was its head that made Rick puke. Its head looked as it if it had been smashed a few times with an axe.

"Christ alive, what do we do now?" Rick said between heaves, he was on his knees puking and GG just looked terrified.

"Look," I said with far more authority than I felt, "I am going to get some help, you guys stay here. I'll be back in ten minutes, look after my stuff."

I dropped the bucket and my fork and with no real idea what to do I started running for help. I knew there wouldn't be any help at home. Dad would just ground me and then in a flash of inspiration I knew exactly where to go. My History teacher, he lived nearer to the beach than anyone I knew, and I presumed he had a phone. I deviated a little and reached the shingle beach, I scrambled up it, across the greensward and within seconds was banging on the door of the cottage he lived in.

Paul Wetherby wasn't fast asleep but he was in a semi-catatonic state in the arms of his wife Francoise, he was putting together a plan of what he could do in the garden today when his daydreaming was shattered by an insistent rapping on his front door. It sounded urgent so Paul roused himself without waking Francoise and slipped his dressing gown and slippers on and made his way through the hall. Opening the door, he was shocked and startled to find Sam Herbert standing there in his wellington boots at 5.30 am. "Sam," he growled. "if this is another of your silly practical jokes I will be speaking to your father later today!" At last the door opened and Mr Wetherby in his dressing gown and slippers and looking rather cross stood there.

"Sir, sir," I puffed, more than a little out of breath. "Sir, it's a body, we've been bait digging but we've found a body, Sir. It's on the beach. We need help."

Mr Wetherby looked at me as if I was mad then made a decision.

"Wait a minute Sam," he said and he turned around partially shutting the front door. Within a minute or two he reappeared with his Wellington boots on and a duffel coat over his pyjamas.

"Very fetching, sir," I sniggered.

"Sam, if you're having me on, I swear you'll regret this, for as long as you live."

"No sir, I am not, promise. This way sir." And I led him back across the greensward and back to the beach.

Following my footsteps in the sand was easy and soon we came into sight of GG & Rick. Rick was standing up by now, with another fag on the go, but they both looked terrified and I have to say more than a little scared of Mr Wetherby.

"Grimes," he said, "those things will kill you in the end. But let's say nothing about it now. At least it takes a little bit of that smell away. I've smelt that before in Normandy and in the Ardennes. That's a rotten corpse boys, a very ripe and well rotten corpse."

He approached the corpse and knelt gingerly beside it . . . he spent a couple of minutes examining it. Then suddenly he stood bolt upright in shock.

"Grimes," he barked. "Have you a telephone at home?" Rick nodded. "Good, go with Green, straight home and dial 999 and ask for the police. Ask to speak to DCI Penrose, he's been dealing with the strange disappearances; tell him that he should get down here right away. Tell him it's urgent, very urgent."

Rick and GG scampered away, running fast.

"What is it, Sir. What have you found."

"You won't believe it Sam," he said. "You won't believe it."

Penrose had just finished a rather nice cooked breakfast in his bachelor pad in Hove. A DCI's wages weren't excessive but he could afford a nice little one bedroom flat with a good sea view. After dropping off Lisa last night he'd got home late and listened to some classical music before going to bed about midnight. He'd woken early shaved and showered and was about to head off to work when the doorbell rang. Lisa stood there looking very summery in a white skirt and blue blouse, she smiled at his surprise.

"Lisa." He sounded astonished. "What are you doing here?"

"Big shout Guv, I was in the office early when we got the call. Some lads in Goring have found a body on the beach and there's a Mr . . ."

She flicked through the pages of her notebook until she found the right page. "Wetherby . . ." she continued.

"Local History teacher, the boys say he's found something significant. We have also had the lab report back about Sean Jackson, just like all the others sir. Throat ripped out and then eviscerated with most of the large organs taken away, no sign of them in the boat. Clear signs of teeth marks on bones and claw marks on some areas of exposed flesh. Death though was from the blow to the back of the head . . . one good thing though, they told me to tell you, no movement post mortem," she added ominously. Penrose moved fast, he gathered the plates and put them in the sink, they would have to wait till later. He grabbed his jacket and tie and on his way out to the car managed to get his tie done up and his jacket on. Lisa got in the driving seat and turned to him with a tissue.

"Excuse me Guv." She laughed and licking the tissue she wiped a smear of egg from the corner of his mouth. Starting the engine, the radio which was already tuned to Radio One blared out "Remember You're a Womble", Penrose rolled his eyes and groaned theatrically. Lisa turned it down and concentrated on driving through the early morning rush hour traffic. They had their break.

Down on the beach I sat on my bucket upwind of the corpse as Mr Wetherby paced back and forward, he was very agitated but he wouldn't tell me why. GG and Rick arrived back and reported to him that had done as instructed, he nodded and said, "Well done," and then went back to his pacing. We sat together and slowly the mist cleared and the morning sun warmed us up. GG still looked awful but Rick's nausea had past.

"You know what it is," GG hissed to us. "It's a Ghoul. I've seen them in my comics. They are dead but they rise up and devour human flesh. The only way to kill them is to chop off their heads. They live in the dark and they kill."

Rick and I looked at each other, and raised our eyebrows, we had both read comics where Ghouls existed but they were comics.

"GG," I hissed back. "They're comics—for goodness sake this is Goring in 1974, not H. P. Lovecraft's Dunwich."

In the distance I could hear the faint sound of a siren and as it got louder and louder we stood up with expectation as the blue lights approached the road beyond the greensward. We heard car doors slam and then two figures appeared at the top of the beach and made their way towards us. One man and a woman, the man was bald and tall and the woman looked really small beside him. She almost was running to keep up with him.

Paul Wetherby realised that it was DCI Penrose from the picture he'd seen in the *Gazette* and he shook hands with him firmly, Penrose introduced DC Lisa Griffin and Paul introduced them both to the lads.

"DCI Penrose, this is Sam." I nodded. "And Rick and Glen and they've something to show you." We realised that we were standing in front of the corpse and with almost theatrical effect we parted and exposed the body for them to see. DC Griffin gasped in shock and Penrose looked grimmer than ever. He moved closer to the corpse and knelt on his hunches besides it. He gazed at the water down by the outfall.

"Thank you boys, forensics are on their way. How much time do we have before the tide reaches us?"

"About ninety minute's sir," I replied. "She's turned about an hour ago and is coming in now." Penrose nodded at me in appreciation.

"So what have we here?" Penrose scratched his chin.

"It's a ghoul," GG shouted out. "It's a ghoul." Rick and I moved to quiet him but Paul interjected and knelt by Penrose.

"There's something very wrong here DCI Penrose, something very wrong."

"Call me Penrose please and what do you mean something's very wrong?"

"Well, for starters I know who this is." We all looked at each other incredulously. "And then there's these."

Paul leaned over the corpse and plucked from the skeletal hand something that glittered in the sunlight. He held it aloft and then slowly lowered it into Penrose's outstretched hand.

"A pair of dog tags." Penrose mused.

"Not just any set of dog tags though Penrose," said Paul rising to his feet. "Look closely at the inscription."

Penrose brought them closer to his eyes and read: "Jackson Sean, Sergeant, Essex Regiment 785903. Bloody hell, that's our last corpse found floating in the boat, well done," he exclaimed. "But who's this fellow then?" He nodded at the corpse on the beach.

"Well, there are a couple of clues. Firstly, how tall do you reckon it is? Six feet eight inches, maybe six ten? He's a tall fella that's for sure, then take a look at its eyes." Penrose turned the head slightly, "What do you see?" Penrose nodded. "And finally there's that tattoo around its neck, I've seen that before, a long time ago when I was at Uni . . ."

The Ambulance and forensic team arrived at that juncture and they took readings and photographs, while we looked quizzically at Mr Wetherby. Of all the people to sound a bit like Sherlock Holmes I never expected it to be Mr Wetherby.

One of the forensic team called Penrose over and we all edged closer to hear what was being said.

"Propeller blade Guv, seen a few of these in my time, you can see the way its sliced into the cranium on a number of occasions."

Rick started to heave again and GG started trembling.

A number of people had started to approach us on the beach, drawn by the large numbers of flashing lights and official looking people. The ambulance crew had managed to get down a slipway about half a mile away and were on their way to us to take away the body.

Penrose asked one of the forensic boys to take some pictures of the tattoo, so I managed to get a good look. It was a serpent, the tail went down the nape of the neck and the body of the beast looped two or three times around the neck before the head appeared just below the left ear. It was grotesque; I'd never seen anything quite like it.

"So tell us about the tattoo please Mr Wetherby?" Penrose spoke quietly but Mr Wetherby looked around him and replied.

"Not here Penrose, I think you'd better come over to my cottage. There's something you need to see."

Penrose nodded and as the ambulance crew started to shift the corpse he barked at the forensic team, "I need a full report on my desk by 2 pm, is that understood." One of them nodded and turned his back, I could hear his cursing and giggled.

"Sam, this is hardly a laughing matter now, is it?" Mr Wetherby rebuked me.

"Lads, you'd better follow us back the Mr Wetherby's, we are going to need statements so we can take them there, if that's okay with you?" He looked at Mr Wetherby who nodded and we set off back up the beach.

There were a lot of inquisitive people but DC Griffin had warned us not to speak a word to anyone and within five minutes we were all seated around a grand dining table in Paul and Francoise's cottage, being served steaming hot tea from porcelain cups and being fed chocolate digestive biscuits.

"Okay, I think before I start that we ought to agree that anything that's said around this table is confidential, I know you're going to have to report to your superiors Penrose but they might not believe what I am going to say. Firstly, though, we need to find out whose boat it was that sliced open our friend on the beach, can you do that?"

Penrose nodded and left the room for a moment to speak to a PC who had accompanied us all back. You could hear the door slam behind him as he went out to do the bidding of his boss. When he'd come back in and settled in his chair Mr Wetherby continued:

"I think we've solved one of the most bizarre mysteries of Anglo-Saxon England today. To be honest though I don't understand it myself yet but I do have some evidence that I want to present to you. My specialism was Anglos Saxon history and in particular the extent of the Viking invasion that took place around 900 BC. One of the most infamous and violent of the Viking pirates was a lad called Ivar the Boneless. We know this because of a famous Anglo-Saxon poem written by one of the people at the court of Athelstan called Eadred, there's one copy left and it's in the British Museum and I've read it. It charts how Athelstan beat the three kings Constantine of the Scots, Eogan of Strathclyde and Olaf Guthfrithson, King of Dublin at the battle of Brunanburh; the poem states categorically that Athelstan would never have won without the strange absence of Olaf's brother; Ivar the Boneless. Ivar was a huge man well over six feet tall, with one eye a different colour to the other and he had a serpent tattoo on his neck. Ivar went missing with his boat and crew on a raid on the south coast of England in 895 AD. and were never seen again."

You could hear a pin drop; I don't think anyone breathed at all for a minute or so. I looked at GG who nodded and at then at Rick who looked green.

"So you're saying our laddie on the beach is a Viking warrior over a thousand years old?" Penrose snorted in disbelief.

"I thought you might say that, so hold on one minute." He went to his sideboard and got a file of papers out. He rummaged around and then with a flourish produced one sheet of A4. "This was from my dissertation, a photocopy of a drawing of the tattoo of Ivar the Boneless, drawn from memory and then handed down through the generations of Norsemen until I found the family in Oslo after the war and they gave me permission to copy it."

There was a sharp intake of breath, it was identical to the one on the body, completely, irrevocably and without doubt, and then we all started talking at once.

GG kept saying, "I told you so, I told you so." Rick was saying: "That's impossible" and finally Penrose banged his fist on the table.

"You're expecting me to go my Chief Super and tell him that the cove who's been killing fisherman for a month now was a dead Viking a thousand years old . . . even worse than that a Viking who eats his victims and leaves them undead?"

"Hang on, what did you say?" I asked as politely as I could. "Are you saying GG is right, that this thing is a Ghoul of some sort?"

Penrose looked slightly abashed. "There's been a few rumours from the coroner's office lad, just a few rumours, nothing to worry about." But I caught the look he gave DC Griffin and I knew there was more to this than he was saying.

Mr Wetherby spoke softly but we were hanging on his every word. "I don't know what it is, you can use the word Ghoul if you like but what we do know is that it killed five people, including our poor Sean Jacobson, until it was hit by a propeller in a fortunate accident. What we have here is a serious situation, there's five men dead, there's going to be a lot more if there are more of these things out there. We need to know the time of death; did you all hear that horrendous noise last night?"

Some of us nodded in turn, reliving that horrible sound, Rick and GG just looked puzzled.

"If Ivar is the last of them then we're out of the woods, if he's not then we've got a serious problem, he had a crew of at least forty-five men on his longboat the infamous Serpent of the North."

There was a rap on the door, we jumped but Penrose took command.

"Come in," he barked and a nervous PC poked his head around the door.

"Guv, seems like a local fisherman name of . . ." He consulted his notebook. '. . . Bertie Brooks had a bit of a collision last night, snapped the cotter pin on his outboard, he's down on the beach fixing it now."

"DC Griffin will be with you shortly," he snapped and the PC closed the door and retreated. "Listen all of you, there's not a word of this to anyone, this could cause panic like nothing we've ever dealt with before. Lisa get off and interview our Bertie and try and pin down the time as best you can. The rest of you stay here until she gets back. Is that clear!"

We nodded as DC Griffin left the room followed by Penrose, who slammed the door behind him.

"Well, lads, it looks like we might be here for a bit! Anyone fancy a game of chess?"

Penrose was in his car speaking to his Chief Superintendent by radio.

"Yes sir, we have a body on the beach that's linked to Sean Jacobson and it looks like he may well have been responsible for the deaths of the four other fishermen too . . . No sir, no formal identification as yet, though we are investigating a number of leads . . . Yes, sir, I'll keep you up to date . . . Thank you sir! Over and out."

Bloody hell, he thought to himself what a bloody mess. He leaned back in the driver's seat and closed his eyes, he might even have drifted off for a moment but was rudely awakened by Lisa rapping on the window.

"Guv, we need to speak with them again."

Mr Wetherby was playing chess with Rick, GG and I was just idly chatting when Penrose and DC Griffin came back into the room.

"I've just interviewed Bertie Brooks and he states quite categorically that he hit something at about 9.30 pm, he remembers it as he wanted to get back in time to watch *Sunday Night at the London Palladium*. He had to row back to shore and he reckons he got to shore at about 10 pm, he pulled his boat up the shingle which took about fifteen minutes and he then heard the most almighty howl from way out at sea and ran home to demolish half a bottle of scotch. Which means; we still got a helluva problem because whatever made that noise out at sea last night wasn't our John Doe known as Ivar the Boneless but some other undead Viking."

We looked at each other, this was suddenly very serious, we had a thousand-year-old dead Viking who'd been eating local fisherman and the likelihood that there might be more of them filled us with dread.

GG suddenly stood up and banged the table.

"It's the Saxon Witch, it's the Saxon Witch," he shouted. "Don't you remember, come on when was it?"

Mr Wetherby nodded and gasped, he quickly went to his sideboard; he rummaged around in a drawer until he returned to his seat with a copy of the *Gazette*.

"Here it is," he said triumphantly. "She was discovered by archaeologists from the University of Sussex in a deep grave on Highdown Hill on April 29th; her remains were uncovered over the next couple of days and were eventually removed on June 3rd. She'd been hung, the hyoid bone was broken which is consistent with being hung, but the weirdest thing was that she was buried with huge boulders of chalk on her legs and arms. It was almost as if whoever buried her wanted her to stay buried for a long, long time. The team at the University state that they've never come across a burial quite like it anywhere. They dubbed her the Saxon Witch, and it's stuck."

"Bloody Hell," hissed Penrose. "Our first victim was found on June 5th, in his boat eviscerated like all the rest, all major organs gone, with bite marks on skin and bones, he was the one that scared that poor lad half to death when he 'woke' in the morgue."

Rick and GG and I all looked at each other with mounting horror.

"There has to be a link between the Saxon Witch and Ivar the Boneless," Rick spoke slowly as if he couldn't really believe he was uttering the words.

I nodded in agreement, "But what the hell could it be?"

At that moment a uniformed PC knocked and stuck his head around the door.

"Guv," he said to Penrose. "It's the Super he wants to see you and DC Griffin asap. He don't sound too happy to be honest," and he raised his eyebrows as if to say 'what's new'.

Penrose and DC Griffin got up to leave but before they went Penrose warned us all about saying anything to anyone, and with that warning ringing in our ears they left us shutting the door behind them as they went.

"Well," said Mr Wetherby, "that's been a Monday morning to remember, I think you lads had better be off back home. Your folks will be wondering where you've been."

I looked over at the clock on the mantelpiece and with astonishment realised it was well after noon. The three of us got up and thanked Mr Wetherby and his wife for the tea and chocolate biscuits and very soon we were outside the cottage heading back towards the beach and our boat. The tide was nearly full by the time we got to it. Mako is a 14-foot dory fishing boat, white fibreglass faux clinker with a transom for the outboard and two rowing stations. We loved it and we spent many hours on the water fishing or just lazing around. The sea was flat calm with just the lightest of waves making that delightful swashing sound and barely a breath of wind. We sat down on the breakwater next to the boat and Rick lit a fag and passed it around. We had a puff or two and passed it back to him.

"Bloody hell," Rick exclaimed. "That's just incredible. What the hell are we going to do now?"

"I am going to go back home," said GG. "Dad will be wanting some help in the shop."

"And you'll be helping yourself to those flying saucers and Sherbet Dips," I giggled and he punched me playfully.

"I think I might wander back too," said Rick. "Tony Blackburn's on Radio 1 at 2 pm, I know he's an arse but there's something about him that makes me smile."

We both nodded, Tony Blackburn was a guilty secret, no-one would admit they liked listening to him but his listening figures were remarkable.

"Okay, lads then I might get on with painting that blasted garden wall," I said with a grimace. That was my chore for the summer chosen by Dad, who else! We lived on a corner plot and the wall was huge, painting it white was an annual thing and the sooner I got started the sooner I'd finish.

"Let's all get together later. Rick is that okay?" Rick nodded and off we went.

When I got home no-one was in so I made a cup of tea, read the newspaper and went out to the shed to get the paint. I found the tin of exterior masonry paint, opened it with a large rather rusty screwdriver and then took a dustsheet and a two-inch paintbrush and went out the front gate. I set the dustsheet down and kneeling began the work. The sun was well up by this time and the temperature was in the eighties. I took off my T-shirt eager to catch some rays, the white paint in the sunshine was blinding after a while and I wished I had some cool sunglasses like Sean seemed to wear all the time. I was just thinking that it was about time for a glass of Corona from the fridge when I was aware of a pair of very, very long and tanned legs beside me. I turned and squinted into the bright sunshine and I was just able to make out that it was Sasha. She looked stunning in a white mini skirt and striped top—a bit like those Frenchman you see in cartoons, but you could immediately see that she was not a man! Incredibly she was holding a copy of Elton John's "Goodbye Yellow Brick Road" which I had heard about but only heard one or two tracks. Long playing records were out of my price range most of the time. It was number one in the album charts over Christmas and I had really wanted it but sadly no-one in my family thought to get it for me.

"Hi Sam," Sasha smiled sweetly at me and I thought I might just pass out with happiness there and then. "I thought you might like to listen to this and tell me what's been going on down at the beach today."

Well, there are times when you don't look a gift horse in the mouth and this was definitely one of them, I nodded, slipped my T-shirt back on; grabbed the tin of paint and the dustsheet and we both went into the garden and to the kitchen door. Like the perfect gentleman I was I opened the door for her and led her through the kitchen into the lounge where the radiogram was. Our radiogram was a sleek looking teak marvel, it stood about two-foot high on four sturdy legs and it had a built in radio and a stereo record player it really was one of the marvels of the day. Dad used to listen to a load of old rubbish on it but it was handy if you wanted to listen to singles or LPs. I asked Sasha if she wanted a drink and when she said yes nipped out to the fridge and came back with some ice-cold lemonade. We sat on a small two seater settee and I gave her a brief run through of the events of the morning. Sasha's eyes widened, and if truth be known became even more gorgeous, as I went through all the gory details, I didn't spare her much. Afterwards I took the record from her, slid it out of the card cover and paper protection sleeve; put it on the turntable and carefully placed the arm over it. As the first track "Funeral for a Friend" filled the room I closed my eyes but it seemed Sasha had other ideas as before I knew it she had leaned over me was kissing me passionately on the lips.

"Sam," she whispered in my ear, "you've known I fancy you haven't you." I nodded trying to look as casual and mature as I could, but to be honest that though had never crossed my mind. By now I had started to respond to her caresses and there was an uncomfortable bulge in my jeans. Sasha noticed but instead of pulling back she slid the zip down and looked at me coyly.

"Do you mind if I touch it?" she whispered. I nodded, fearing that very soon I was going to wake up from this delightful dream.

"Blimey Sam," she giggled as she gripped it tight. "Supersam the Man of Steel." And she wasn't wrong it was like a rod of iron. I moved around a bit awkwardly at first but I eventually managed to slide her knickers down and before we knew it we were involved in some serious heavy petting. I don't think I've ever touched something so soft, so warm and so moist in my life, before or since.

Then we heard two car doors slam.

Superintendent Cameron McDonald stood behind his desk glowering at Penrose and DC Griffin. He stood in front of the window of the 6th floor office with the whole of Brighton and Hove beach silhouetted behind him, the view was truly awesome. He'd been ranting at the pair of them for a good ten minutes and was beginning to tire.

Penrose didn't care about the view though what he cared about was being roasted by a wet behind the ears posh boy who looked as if he's had a steel rod shoved up his jacksie, DC Griffin just thought he looked a prat. A small man of military bearing McDonald sported a rather pathetic black moustache that made him look a bit like Adolf Hitler, though no one ever told him that to his face, but many's the time he'd be strutting around the grand and rather palatial CID Headquarters in Brighton and he'd hear someone whistling "Hitler has only got one ball" he never challenged it just ignored it.

"Just what are you two telling me," he roared with his piggy eyes bulging from his reddened and enraged face. "That we've got a thousand-year-old Viking going around killing people in Goring and that he might have accomplices. Are you truly mad, have you completely lost the plot; if this gets out we will be a laughing stock and worst of all my chance of a knighthood will be blown away."

The only thing Cameron McDonald really cared for was this prospective knighthood, and the masons of which he was Grand Master.

"Sir," Penrose interjected, "the evidence . . ."

"Evidence, there is no bloody evidence at all, just the gibberish of a bunch of stupid schoolboys and a soppy History teacher who should know better. I want a press release this afternoon saying that an itinerant has been found dead in Goring and the police have reason to believe his is the person responsible for the deaths of five fishermen." He banged his fist forcefully on the table. "Do I make myself clear," he added with real menace.

Penrose and DC Griffin looked at each other, Penrose sighed and nodded and they both left the office leaving Cameron McDonald to slump back to his seat and catch his breath. He had a Masonic do tonight and he wanted to be at his best. He didn't need these stupid trivialities ruing his life.

I froze and my erection disappeared in seconds, Sasha looked at me alarmed, and if I may say so, a little disappointed.

"Quick," I pointed and said quietly, "through the French doors and out the side gate, I'll see you later." She pecked me on the cheek and disappeared through the doors as the kitchen door opened. Mum and Dad made their way into the lounge where I stood sheepishly in front of the radiogram.

"What the hell have you been up to?" Dad glowered at me. "What happened to the fishing and what's going on with the painting."

Mum raised her eyebrows at me and nodded in the direction of my feet. I glanced down as if I was abashed and to my horror saw a pair of black, lacy knickers draped over my Converse.

"Bloody hell," I roared, "who the hell is that," and pointed at the French doors and as they both spun to look I quickly grabbed the knickers and tucked them in the pocket of my jeans doing up my flies seconds later.

"Sorry," I said as they both turned to me in astonishment. "I thought I saw someone in the garden, been a bit too long in the sun today." I stammered an apology.

Dad looked at me shrewdly, he knew something was amiss but he couldn't quite get what. I knew I had to be careful.

"Who the hell is that singing? If you can call it singing," he sneered. Elton was just getting into "Jamaica Jerk Off" which was going to annoy him on so many levels.

"It's Elton John dad, it's the LP I wanted for Christmas, a friend lent it to me and I thought I'd listen to a few tracks before carrying on with the painting."

"Elton bloody John, is it." His voice dripped with malice, "The man's a poofter I've read all about him in the papers. Never thought I'd see the day when a son of mine would be listening to a bloody homosexual." He almost spat the last word out.

"Charles," Mum intervened, "that's quite enough swearing from both of you for one day, why don't you go and make some tea please."

He turned abruptly and went off, muttering about poofters and black music and god knows what else; very soon we heard the tap go on as he filled the kettle and put it on the hob. Mum looked at me and smiled knowingly.

"Sam," she said quietly, "I hope you aren't taking risks please, I hope you are taking *precautions.*" She over emphasised the word for my benefit.

"Mum, I know exactly what I am doing, we've done all that stuff at school," I said with much more confidence that I felt. Our sex education consisted of one fifty-minute lesson which mainly involved an embarrassed and increasingly tetchy elderly male teacher a cucumber and a condom and about 30 boys making increasingly ribald and rude comments. In the end the condom split and the teacher left the classroom in a huff before the bell went.

"Well I hope so! One mistake and you can be trapped you know, trapped for a long, long time." At that moment all I wanted to do was to hug her and tell her that everything would be all right but I couldn't. You just didn't do that sort of thing in our family. She looked at me with real fear in her eyes then turned without saying another word and left the room.

I turned off the record and put it back in its sleeve and left it on the side. I hoped that Sasha would be back to listen to the rest of the record quite soon. I particularly wanted to listen to "Dirty Little Girl" with her in my arms.

It stirred, it was hungry, it was aware it was alone but most of all it wanted revenge. Revenge on those who caused this to happen. Slowly it got to its feet and attacked the inside of its cage with heavy blows on the timbers that enclosed him. Once it had smashed the hull of the upturned longboat it clawed its way through the hard packed sand until it emerged on the sea bed. It got its bearings and headed towards the shore. It was looking for a place of sanctuary and it found the storm drain and crawled into it, heading away from the sea and towards the people.

"Berty" Brooks was pissed; he'd been in the pub most of the day trying to forget about that horrendous howl and the terrors it had stirred within him. Drinking pints of mild and bitter with whisky chasers he tried to chase away the demons he'd had since the war. It didn't work and in the end the barman had refused to serve him anymore so here he was slumped on the bench outside the churchyard, opposite the pub trying to sleep it off. The sun was out and the mosquitoes buzzed around him as he snored fitfully. He didn't hear the drain cover being shoved open from below, he didn't hear the drain cover being slid away from the drain, he didn't hear the thing that emerged from beneath the road but the smell hit him hard. He'd smelled that stench before in the Ardennes, rotting putrid flesh, he struggled to sit up and then started screaming as he saw the thing that had appeared before him. A skeletal monster with a cavernous maw full of sharp teeth with breath that stank of the charnel house reared above him and then struck. His screams continued until the thing ripped his throat out, it fed quickly and then slipped back into the storm drain. Some of the regulars heard the screams and tumbled blearily out into the car park. They saw the blood spattered body; the barman returned to the bar to call for the police whilst some of the regulars teetering a bit from their early evening drinks moved towards the body and then stopped in horror as it twitched once or twice and then rose from the bench inhumanely howling. It turned towards them and started lurching towards them; their terrified and panic stricken flight back towards the pub was instant. The creature picked up speed running with a palpable air of menace as it ran across the road .

. . only to be hit by the Number 19 bus. The driver white with shock halted the bus with the terrified passenger screaming as they were thrown around by the emergency stop. Shaking with trauma he got out of the cab and then vomited copiously into the kerb as he saw the trapped torso under the wheels, hissing and spitting and trying to grab him with the rest of the things bloody remains lying some fifteen feet behind it, a trail of gore linked the two halves of the body.

Penrose and DC Griffin arrived about ten minutes later; they got the call from the same ambulance crew that had dealt with the body on the beach that morning. Penrose had phoned McDonald and they were waiting for him impatiently. The cordon had been set up by the local Bobbies to exclude nosy locals as well as some of the press that had managed to find out about the accident. Penrose had instructed the ambulance crew to leave the scene of the accident exactly as it was. He wanted his Superintendent to see this for what it was, eventually a black Daimler screeched to a halt by the edge of the cordon and McDonald resplendent in black uniform, cap and medals emerged. He marched with purpose over to Penrose and DC Griffin.

"This had better be worth my while Penrose, I was on my way to a Masonic do in Hove, and you call me over here to a road traffic accident . . . you'd better not be wasting my time."

"Yes sir." Penrose was breathing deeply to control his anger. "Just thought you'd like to take a look at this. The body of one 'Berty' Brooks one of our local fishermen." He pulled aside the screen and beckoned McDonald through. McDonald stepped inside and Penrose let the screen flap shut behind him.

After the initial sharp intake of breath, they heard nothing until McDonald emerged a minute or so later, looking as white as a sheet and visibly perspiring. He barely looked at Penrose and DC Griffin striding purposefully past them to his limousine. He pulled open the door and barked instructions to his driver. As he pulled away McDonald lowered the window and when the car was level with the two police officers he said: "You two, my office, tomorrow morning, full coroner's report and an explanation."

As the black Daimler accelerated away Penrose and Lisa exchanged knowing glances and shook their heads. Penrose nodded to the ambulance crew who were getting ready to deal with the twitching remains.

What Penrose, McDonald and DC Griffin were completely unaware of were the four pairs of eyes staring down at the scene from the among the leafed branches of the giant oak tree in the corner of the churchyard. GG had heard the commotion and rung the other three in quick succession. I was running to my bike even as I put the phone down and we met beneath the ancient tree and scaled it as we had done so many times before. Now I sat astride one of the mighty branches legs dangling over the void. Rick had brought his Instamatic camera with him and was snapping pictures of the scene displayed below us. GG was hanging on like grim death and panting with the exhaustion of both the race here and the rapid ascent of the tree. Sean looked on faintly amused and slightly bewildered as we had only managed to fill him in piecemeal on the events of the morning but even he gasped when Superintendent McDonald sunk to one knee as he saw the savage feral beast trapped beneath the wheels of the bus and then he staggered to his feet before making his unsteady way to the rest of the body a long way behind shaking his head and wiping his brow in obvious discomfort.

"Christ alive, I've seen it all now," said Rick shaking his head in disbelief, "is that what I think it is?"

"Yep, I told you so," GG retorted, "a bloody Ghoul, a real live bloody Ghoul, if it bites you, you become the same, a slavering inhuman wretch condemned forever to lust after human flesh."

"I've done a bit of that in my time." Sean smirked and looked directly at me. I blushed under his gaze and turned back as the ambulance crew entered the closed off area. They gingerly approached the snarling remains until one of them produced a scalpel and lunged at the thing, it pierced its ear and sank into the cranium, it stopped moving immediately and you could sense the feeling of relief amongst the crew as they went about their grisly task.

I pointed out the blood soaked bench and the trail of gore and blood that you could see going back to the open drain cover.

"That's how it got here; it's gone into the bloody storm drain. There are miles and miles of that, no one's safe." Rick looked a bit panicky.

"We need to show these pictures to Mr Wetherby," said GG, "he'll know what to do next and he has a darkroom I saw it when we were in the cottage, it's just a cupboard but it's got the red light outside, I sneaked a quick peek in there this morning."

"Well done, Watson," I said in my best Sherlock Holmes accent, "let's get a move on then before that bloody thing comes back for more food."

We shinned down the tree and picked up our bikes, then set off pedalling hell for leather to Mr Wetherby's cottage.

Later that evening a group of University students were having a party on the beach. They were all from the local sixth form who had returned from the four corners of the country after their first year and were having a reunion of sorts on the beach. Someone had lit a fire in a pit made by scooping out the pebbles on the beach, potatoes were baking in the ashes and a ready supply of driftwood had been found to keep the fire going till late. A couple of Party Sevens had been opened and bottles of Scrumpy cider were being consumed with relish. Rolled up cigarettes were being passed around and a good time was being had by all as exaggerated stories of fresher week madness were related around the fire. Molly Bellchamber sat apart from the main group of students, she was missing her boyfriend, Simon, who'd she'd met at fresher's week and they'd been inseparable ever since. The trouble was Simon lived in Liverpool and they'd had a tearful parting at Cardiff railway station a few days previously. Now Molly sat just above the water line, her toes being tickled by the gentle swash as she absent-mindedly threw stones into the dark deep and mysterious waters of the English Channel. It wasn't just the wood smoke that was bringing tears to her eyes but the thought of Simon her first love all those miles away.

In the Masonic Temple a few miles away on the border of Worthing and Shoreham Superintendent McDonald was sitting in the oak panelled and opulent bar sipping steadily from his fourth Scotch of the night but the buzz from the alcohol was barely touching the deep anxiety he felt after witnessing the scene at the road traffic accident earlier in the day. He sensed that this was well beyond his capabilities; he doubted that anyone could deal with this, certainly not someone who might have been promoted beyond his ability; he felt out of depth and not for the first time in his life frankly lost. The tap on his shoulder dragged him from his maudlin thoughts, he turned and smiled and reached for the outstretched hand.

"Cameron, lovely to see you here, how's things?" said his fellow Mason.

"Not too bloody good, got a bit of situation in your neck of the woods I am afraid. Bunch of bloody schoolboys and some lefty bloody History teacher seem to have an idea that there's a bloody Viking going around killing people. It's caused a helluva stir, I am trying to keep it under wraps but if this gets out I'll be a laughing stock."

"A bunch of bloody schoolboys eh? One of them wouldn't be Sam Herbert?" the Mason enquired in a hushed voice.

"Yes, he's one of the little bastards, a Herbert eh? Is he a relation of yours by any chance? Going around upsetting local people, I wouldn't be surprised if we arrested the lot of 'em for wasting police time."

"No that won't be necessary Cameron, I think I'll deal with this one."

Charles Herbert polished off his drink with a single gulp and slammed the glass on the table so violently he damn near broke the glass. He turned on his heels and stormed out of the room, leaving Superintendent McDonald wondering what the hell had got him so wound up and pitying anyone who crossed Charles tonight. His reputation for a short fuse went before him.

Molly smiled as she recognised Bryan Ferry's distinctive voice echoing from a tinny transistor by the fire "I'm in with the 'in' crowd" he sang, but Molly didn't feel part of any crowd tonight. All she wanted was to hear Simon's voice again. He'd promised to phone her every day and true to his word he'd phoned her this morning but she wished she could hear his voice one more time tonight.

The moon was shining brightly and the reflection on the water was gorgeous, Molly started as she saw a v-shaped ripple coming rapidly towards the shore. It seemed to be heading straight for where she was sitting. Molly hadn't drunk much or smoked any of the weed being passed around otherwise she might not have been so lucky. As it approached she stumbled to her feet, the shingle nearly betraying her as she slipped and screamed in terror as the head of the beast broke water about ten yards off shore. It moved menacingly and unerringly directly towards her. The scream alerted the others by the fire and they gasped in terror as they saw the monstrous apparition bearing down on Molly. Some of them grabbed pebbles and started flinging them in the direction of the beast whilst others snatched flaming branches and driftwood from the edge of the fire pit and moved as one towards the water's edge. The barrage of stones and the wall of fire seemed to confuse the beast and it turned, howled in pain and frustration and sank back beneath the waves. Molly found herself in the arms of a handsome, muscular bearded lifeguard named Brian, and all of a sudden she forgot about Simon from Liverpool.

Tonight was turning out to be not too bad a night at all.

I was lying in bed reading *Orphans of the Sky* by Robert Heinlein when I heard the car screech into the drive and the door slam. We'd all cycled to Mr Wetherby's earlier and explained to him what we'd seen from the branches of the great oak tree, it was an excited rabble that turned up at his doorstep but with good humour and a little calm direct questioning he managed to get the whole story from us as we sat around his dining room table. He took copious notes as his wife Francoise, stared at us with astonishment and growing fear as we relayed everything we'd seen. He agreed to develop the film for us and as it was getting late he ushered us to the door and urged us all to go straight home. He shut the door firmly behind us and we heard a number of locks and bolts being clicked into place as we picked up our bikes from the lawn where we'd abandoned them earlier.

"What now," said Sean with some bravado. "Are we all going ghoul hunting."

"Not me," I said. "I've had enough of this for one day, we were up really early this morning and we never got our bait, I am knackered. I don't know about you lot but I need my beauty sleep!"

GG and Rick giggled, but nodded their approval. It had been an extraordinarily long day. So we agreed to meet around Rick's after breakfast the following day. I climbed aboard the old Raleigh and cycled the short distance home, popped the bike in the shed and made way upstairs. Mum's light was off and Dad was out, so I cleaned my teeth and settled down with Robert Heinlein. The back door slammed beneath me with some force, and I sat up a little straighter in my bed. That sounded a little ominous.

"Sam, get down here right now." The shouted command was clear and unequivocal, he'd been drinking and he was mad, really mad!

"Sam, now, right now!" he bellowed. Slowly I got to my feet and opened the bedroom door onto the landing. Mum's door opened and she came out, looking bewildered and nervous, her hair in rollers and wearing the pink dressing gown and silly furry slippers I got for her last Christmas.

"Charles, come to bed, the boys asleep he's had a long day. Let me make you a cup of tea."

"I've never been so embarrassed in my entire life," he roared. "The bloody Grand Master of my Lodge complains to me about my boy and I know nothing whatsoever about it . . . have you any idea what that means?" His voice rose another notch or two in volume and it sounded like he'd punched the wall in anger.

"Sam, if you don't come down here then I am coming to get you . . . and you wouldn't want that now . . . would you?" the question was laced with menace and violence.

"Charles stop it now, you're scaring the boy, don't be so silly come upstairs."

"Oh, I am coming up there now," he cried and launched himself at the stairs taking them two at a time. Mum tried to defend me from him but he brushed her aside in his drunken fury. I saw her grab the banister and then her hand slipped with the violence of the assault and she simply pivoted and fell. The noise was horrendous, two heavy bumps and a crash and then total and utter silence.

Dad suddenly realised what he'd done, he stopped and turned and as he did so, I took my opportunity and ran past him, he tried to grab me but I was too quick, I was down the stairs and through the kitchen and out the back door in a flash.

"You little bastard," he screamed in fury, "you see what you've made me do."

I ran and ran, I could barely see through the tears that were running freely down my face. I didn't know where to go; I was barefoot in pyjamas, it was dark, I was alone and scared. Scared of my family and scared of whatever was in the storm drain. I couldn't knock on the doors of my friends as they were all asleep and to be honest I didn't want them to know about what just happened. I got to the beach, in the distance I could see a bonfire and a group of people having a whale of time, I heard their laughter and their music, carried along the shore by the light sea breeze. I stumbled along the foreshore until I reached our boat; I lifted the tarpaulin cover and crept inside. I pulled the cover back over and snuggled down under the seat using one of the old lifejackets as a pillow I fell into a deep and dreamless sleep. The screams from the bonfire party and the subsequent shouting and hullabaloo didn't bother me one bit.

It came back ashore still looking for prey; it shuffled along the foreshore scenting the light breeze. It was near. It could smell it, but then the scent got lost and all it could smell was rotten fish. It gave up and returned to the sea, back to its lair in the labyrinth of storm drains that ran for miles beneath the sleeping town.

Andrew Newcombe was woken by the gentle sound of his puppy whimpering in the hall below. Andrew lived in his aunt's old house about two hundred metres from the sea. She'd died and he'd been left the house in her will. Andrew had lived there for about fourteen years with his long-time partner, Mo. Andrew and Mo worked for the Inland Revenue, they had large offices a mile or so away by the station. Being a gay couple in 1974 wasn't something you shouted from the rooftops so to the outside world Mo was Andrew's lodger and bachelor friend. Their first dog, a lovely black Labrador named Bouncer had died before Christmas last year and they had delayed getting another but in the end emotion had won out and now they had a new puppy called Yorker, to continue the cricketing theme, another black Lab which was slowly getting house trained. Andrew glanced at the clock on the bedside table and raised his eyebrows in mock horror as he saw 2:15 on the dial. Mo was gently snoring beside him so quietly he got out of bed, slipped on his black leather slippers and grabbed a paisley print dressing gown from the hook on the bedroom door. Yorker was whining by the front door so Andrew slipped on the lead and led the dog down the path to the gate. It squeaked loudly as he opened it and the pair of them set foot onto the pavement. The grass verge beckoned to Yorker and the pair set off slowly walking between the cones of orange light lit by the streetlamps, it was mild and calm, a bat flickered between the streetlamps as they made their way slowly along. Yorker sniffed at everything and seemed set on doing his business when he suddenly froze. Andrew, still holding the lead, was pulled up short. He heard the clang of the storm drain cover and smelt the putrid graveyard stench that emanated from it. He turned slowly, sensing that something monstrous was behind him, his legs shaking with fear and when he saw the apparition his mouth opened in a silent scream, the thing struck and Andrew fell, within seconds all that remained on the pavement was a cowering puppy shaking with terror and a single solitary leather slipper.

Chapter 3: Tuesday

I awoke with a horrifying start as the tarpaulin was slowly pulled away from the top of the boat; my heart was in my mouth as I expected the Ghoul to appear above me, so when I looked up into Rick & GG's stupid faces I almost wept with joy.

"There you are you silly sod." Rick smiled, "We've been looking for you since the cops came round at 6 am. There's been an accident and your mum's in hospital . . . hang on . . . why are you still in your pyjamas?"

"It's a long story, a very long story," I said as I eased myself upright, sleeping in the boat had been good but I was a stiff as a board. Muscles creaked and joints popped as I managed to sit up on one of the seats and then haul myself over the gunwale and onto the shingle.

"You'd better come back to mine," said Rick so GG and I followed him back up the road to his mum's house, where I was greeted with some incredulity by his mum, who sat me down in the kitchen and offered up loads of Typhoo tea and toasted Hovis and Marmite.

The radio was on and the local news was describing an incident by the shore last night as well as the tragic death of 'Bertie' Brooks in a road traffic accident. We looked at each other with bewilderment when that was mentioned. At the end of the news the DJ launched into "Shang-A-Lang" by the Bay City Rollers and we all groaned in disgust, GG pretended to vomit on the table.

There was a rap on the door and Sean arrived brandishing the local paper. With a flourish he laid it on the table before us and we all stared at the images on the front page. It seems a local newshound had snapped a few pictures of the scene and sold them on. There was one picture in particular that caught my eye, two huge bloodied hand prints on the trunk at the foot of the great oak where we'd been hiding and taking our own pictures.

"There's something about that tree," I mused. "There's something about the Saxon Witch and there's something about our Viking Ghoul. If we could put it together we might be able to end this here and now. I think it's time we paid our History teacher another visit."

The lads nodded in approval and Rick told me to go up to his room to get changed. He was roughly the same size as me, so I threw on a pair of flared jean, a tie-dyed T-shirt and pair of old white plimsolls that just about fitted me. I was about to go back downstairs when a tap at the door made me pause.

"Come in," I said and Mrs Grimes poked her head around the door.

"Sam, hold on a minute. There's something I need to tell you." She spoke quietly almost reverentially. "It's your mum." I gasped and with that she rushed over to me and hugged me tight. "No, Sam, she's alright, it's the baby. She lost the baby." And then she started sobbing uncontrollably in my arms. "I know she wanted the baby too." She sniffed between sobs. "It'll break her heart; you'll have to be strong for her now."

"I will be," I reassured her. "But now we've got a huge problem on our hands and it's up to us to sort it out."

I gave her a final squeeze and made my way downstairs, my anger was immense, an internal rage against my old man and against the thing that had created all these problems. My fury knew no bounds at that point, I needed settlement. My bike had miraculously appeared courtesy of GG.

"There was no-one home." He shrugged nonchalantly and with that the four of us set off back to Mr Wetherby's cottage by the sea.

Penrose and DC Griffin sat opposite each other at their respective desks in the incident room. Both were bashing away at typewriters as if their life depended on it, when a PC coughed loudly and handed Penrose a piece of paper.

Penrose scanned it and said to DC Griffin, "Another incident on the beach last night, seems a party got interrupted by our old sea loving friend, luckily there were enough people around to see him off and he's not been seen since. It only got reported this morning after someone saw the pictures of our 'Road Traffic Accident'," he said in a voice laced with irony.

"Most of these bloody incidents take place at night, so what made it come up out of the storm drain and eviscerate poor old Bertie in the afternoon? It just doesn't make much sense Guv, does it?"

"We've also had a report of a domestic involving one of our witnesses," continued Penrose. "It seems that Sam Herbert's mum fell down the stairs last night. Sam's missing and his dad is at Worthing hospital with mum creating merry hell. Telling everyone that he knows Cameron McDonald and there will be hell to pay if we don't find him, pretty damn quick. I tell you I've been thinking long and hard about this case Lisa, six deaths, one suspect dead, and another one at large. I've a half mind to close the beaches and tell people to stay indoors, but it would freak the Super out completely."

Lisa Griffin continued the litany of bad news, "Another caller, a Mr Mohammed Ashraf, says his landlord, Andrew Newcombe is missing. He woke up at 6.30 to find the front door ajar and the puppy gone as well. I've sent two PCs to have a look, they found the puppy shaking with fear and one of Mr Newcombe's slippers by a land drain. Blood spatters everywhere."

"Guv," a PC interrupted him calling across the incident room, "just had a call from a Mrs Grimes to say that Sam Hebert is all right, it seems he spent the night sleeping on the beach! He's with Mrs Grimes now having come breakfast."

"That's some good news at least. I want to know about anything unusual that's happening in Goring, however bizarre or stupid. Got that?" The PC nodded at Penrose and returned to the mound of paperwork on his desk.

Penrose rose with a sigh and he and DC Griffin left the incident room for another trip to the beach.

Penrose and DC Griffin stared at the remains of the beach party with some amusement, the fire was smouldering and wood smoke lifted slowly into the clear morning air. The area around the fire pit was littered with bottles and cans and here and there a soggy condom lay trapped between two pebbles.

"At least they were taking precautions." Lisa grinned, looking on in delight at the grimace of distaste plastered over Penrose's face.

"It seems the party was disturbed by something that came from the sea, and they managed to beat it off with pebbles and fire. Quite remarkable that this bunch of bloody drippy students survived an attack by that thing." Penrose gazed at the vast expanse of the sand exposed by the low tide. "It really does beggar belief."

On their way back to the car DC Griffin grabbed Penrose's arm and pointed to four cyclists tearing along the road towards them.

"That's Sam Herbert in front on that green bike." She started running towards the road.

"Sam, hold up," she hollered and slowly the quartet slowed down and as she reached the road they pulled into the kerb.

Seconds later Penrose arrived, panting and looking a tad peeved that Griffin had beaten him to it by a fairly long way.

On the way to Mr Wetherby's the two coppers, Penrose and Griffin, saw us from the beach, they flagged us down by the side of the road Griffin arrived first followed by Penrose who looked a bit puffed after his exertions and started to speak to all of us.

"Lads," he said after he got his breath back, "we had another incident last night, it seems our Viking friend wanted a bit of party action last night, one girl only escaped by the skin of her teeth as a group of lads beat the thing back with flaming brands. Honestly it's probably best if you keep away from the beach . . . for a few days at least."

We looked at each other knowingly, he didn't know that we knew what was really going on.

"Sam," he continued looking right at me. "Your dad's at the Hospital with your mum, he's worried sick, you need to get down there asap. Okay?"

I nodded. "Yes DCI Penrose, I am off there in just a minute. I've just got to pick up some bits from Sean's and then I am on my way."

"Good lad." Penrose smiled at me. "Go on then you rascals, get off home and keep yourselves safe."

Slowly we pedalled off and as soon as we were a good distance away I shouted at the others.

"To Wetherby's lads, I've got a plan."

"You want what, Sam? You must be joking; they won't lend that to me. I am just a humble History teacher these boys are professional archaeologists." Mr Wetherby looked at me as if I was stark raving bonkers. "You honestly think they'd let me have the Saxon Witch's skull, even for half a day?"

"Sir," I pleaded with him, "for the plan to work we need to lure the thing out of the storm drain. I believe it's got some sort of link to Goring, some sort of link to that oak tree and a definite link to the Saxon Witch. If we can get it out of the storm drain, then we can deal with it."

"Sam even if I could these things have killed before and they're itching to kill again. What's to stop us not becoming more of its victims or even ending up like poor old 'Bertie' brooks." He shuddered. Mr Wetherby had processed the reel of photos that we had taken and he and Francoise had examined them in detail. What they showed was something beyond his comprehension.

GG interrupted. "Sir, Sam's plan is a good one. We have to try for the sake of everyone in Goring. If that thing strikes again and Ghoul infects others we could have a full scale catastrophe. The like of which we've never seen before. I've seen the *Night of the Living Dead* sir, and it ain't pretty. Thousands of infected victims stalking the living in a desperate bid to spread the infection. It could well be the end of the world."

"I agree," Rick butted in, "we are the only ones who seem to be aware of the danger. Penrose and Griffin seem to think it's just going to go away but it won't if we don't do something then Goring is going to go down in history as the place the world started to come to an end."

Sean had his sixpenny worth too. "I've read Richard Matheson's *I am Legend* and that's what we have here. If it gets out there won't be a single person on the planet who won't be affected."

Mr Wetherby looked in exasperation for help to his wife Francoise who sat at the end of the table. We all looked at her expectantly. She looked back at each and every one of us before she turned to Mr Wetherby.

"Paul, the boys are right," she said in a delightful French accent. "Great evil like this must be confronted. That's what you did in Normandy and that's what you must do again today."

Mr Wetherby shook his head and then stood abruptly, he walked to the telephone, got out his notebook, skimmed a few pages and then dialled the number. A long mumbled conversation took place before we heard Mr Wetherby say: "That's great, many thanks. I will be over in half an hour to pick it up."

He returned to the table and slumped into his chair.

"Right that's it. I am driving over to Brighton to pick it up. I've told them I want to make some sketches for my A level class next year. I've got to get it back by tomorrow morning. Sam if this goes wrong I'll lose my job, this cottage and everything I've worked for. This had better work."

"Oh, it will sir," I said triumphantly, but there was part of me thinking that this could all go terribly wrong.

We agreed to meet at noon to set the plan in motion and we waved Mr Wetherby off in his green Austin A60 on his short drive to Sussex University.

The four of us returned to Rick's garage where we set about finalising our plan.

"GG, Sean and Rick, I want you to go to four different garages and get jerry cans of fuel. We'll need it if we're going to flush this beast out. We'll also need one of those seine nets that we got last summer. I think they are in my garage so I am going to get it. We all okay?"

"We'll need some money," Rick said.

"Bloody good point, hang on." I jumped on my bike and cycled the short distance to my house. The key was under the flowerpot and I let myself in through the front door. There was an ugly blood stain on the floor at the bottom of the stairs which I avoided with some dexterity and distaste and I made my way up the stairs to my bedroom. On the bookcase was my secret money box, I'd hollowed out a copy of Robinson Crusoe just for an emergency like this. Inside were my wages from the paper round and cash from other odd jobs I'd done around the place. There must have been nigh on twenty quid in there and I pocketed the lot.

I was saving up for a new fishing reel, but I reckoned saving the world might come slightly ahead of that. I quickly changed into some of my own clothes, a pair of 501s and a tie-died T-shirt courtesy of Worthing Market and I got the seine net out of the shed brushed off the cobwebs and mice droppings and returned to the garage. I handed out the cash and the lads sped off in different directions.

I spent a few minutes gathering five old Coca Cola bottles and filling them up with fuel from the outboard motor tank that we kept in the garage I stuffed rags into the tops of the bottles and stood back to admire my work. Five little Molotov cocktails ready for action.

I looked at the tide table pinned to the wall by the outboard motor, we were going to have to time this right otherwise the tide would scupper the plan and we'd be in mortal danger. I spread a map of Goring out on the table in front of me and I started to plan where we'd need to start driving the beast towards the Saxon Witch and its eventual doom.

Suddenly, someone placed very soft hands over my eyes and kissed me on the back of the neck! The pleasure that brought me was electric.

"Guess who, Iron Sam?" the voice whispered in my ear as is owner gently nuzzled my earlobes with their tongue.

"Sasha, is that you?" I gasped, I literally could barely speak.

"Who d'ya think it was?" she giggled coquettishly as she came around and stood in front of me. Sasha was dressed in a white peasant smock top that was as near as damn it see-through and a gorgeously tight pair of distressed Levi's. She looked a million dollars. "I waited until the others had left, I thought you might not appreciate me coming in while the boys are around?" She looked at me with those dark brown eyes smouldering from under her long eyelashes and my knees buckled slightly.

I kissed her long and deep, crushing her to me with passion. I could feel her heart pounding through my chest and I just lost myself in the moment.

A loud cough dragged me back to reality for there standing in the doorway was my dad. Boy he looked worse for wear, I could see his stubble growing through on his chin, his hair was dishevelled and unkempt and his tie was hanging from his neck in a most ungainly manner. I reckon he'd been drinking again but I wasn't going to make the mistake of getting too close to find out.

"Sam." His voice was hoarse and croaky with emotion, but I wasn't sure if it was remorse or anger. "I've just come from the hospital. Your mum lost the baby."

I moved to put myself between Sasha and my dad, I had a feeling he was on the edge again and I would do anything to stop her getting hurt by anyone.

"I know." The edge in my voice was clear. "Last night you blamed me, or have you forgotten already?"

I heard the intake of breath from Sasha behind me.

He sagged visibly and grabbed hold of the back of one of the deck chairs for support, he looked and sounded a broken man.

"Your mum is divorcing me, I've just come by to pick up a few things from the house and I'm off to stay with my sister in Bexhill for a few days. We're going to sort out the divorce and she's going to keep the house. I'll make arrangements to ensure you don't suffer."

"Any more?" I snorted with derision.

"I know, I know, I've been a bad father and it's time for me to move on, let you and your mum find yourselves. I am an idiot and I regret everything."

He turned and lurched down the drive to the road and headed back to our house. I heard the clang of the storm drain cover and even as I started to run towards him he screamed and stumbled. Reaching the end of the drive I turned to see him disappearing at a rate of knots down into the storm drain. By the time I got to the storm drain his hands were the only thing left of him on the surface. I tried to pull him back up but with an almighty scream he vanished from view. His face, illuminated in the tunnel from the light of the sun, looked at me from the depths imploringly and then vanished as the creature pulled him away in a flourish of activity. I stood, shivering with shock, as Sasha approached me cautiously.

"What was that?" she asked her voice trembling in fear. I put my arms around her and stared at the sea beyond the greensward.

"It's a problem that we have to stop today!" I said with steel in my voice. She shuddered against me.

At that moment a battered green A60, tooted and pulled up alongside us, Mr Wetherby got out, he went to the boot and on opening it handed me a small box crate, packed with straw. I lifted the lid and nestled safely within was the skull of the Saxon Witch.

"That's it," said Mr Wetherby, I've got to get it back to them by noon tomorrow. "Sam, you've got to look after it."

I nodded in agreement and took it into the relative safety of the garage. Mr Wetherby revved the car and disappeared home leaving us to our own devices. The plan was beginning to take shape, but as a responsible adult I didn't think it would do Mr Wetherby any good at all to be associated with it. Sean, Rick and GG turned up about five minutes later with steel the jerry cans strapped precariously to the rack on each of their bikes and we sat around the table I outlined the plan.

"Sean, Rick and GG I want you three to go to these locations." I pointed at the map. "It's midday now and at 12.35 exactly I want you to pour those jerry cans of fuel down the storm drain and throw in one of these." I held up one of the Molotov cocktails rather proudly. "I reckon our friend hasn't gone any further than the tree in the church and these three points are upstream from there so the burning fuel will flush him towards me and Sasha at the storm drain on the beach. At the same time, I am sure that it will be attracted by the lure of my little friend here."

I tapped the box on the table and lifted the lid to display the skull of the Saxon Witch. There were gasps of approval and astonishment from the three lads.

"When it emerges I am going to drop the net on it and then we can deal with it with another couple of my little Molotovs. It's as easy as that." I smiled, with a lot more bravado and confidence than I actually felt.

Penrose and DC Griffin had just left a distraught Mo Ashraf crying on the leather sofa in the well decorated living room of the house he had shared with Andrew Newcombe cuddling Yorker and sobbing uncontrollably. He'd not really been able to supply any more details as he'd slept right through it and he only realised that there might have been an issue when he woke up when the alarm went off to an empty bed.

They were heading back to Hove along the A27 when the car radio squeaked into life.

"Guv," the disembodied voice echoed around the Triumph, "we've just had two or three separate reports of lads pouring petrol into the storm drains in Goring and setting the fuel on fire . . . you said to let you know of anything unusual . . . Guv?"

Penrose and Griffin exchanged glances and Penrose shook his head in disgust.

"Okay cheers," he snapped at the radio. "What are those bloody idiots up to?" he snarled as he spun the car through 180 degrees with tyres squealing in protest and set off back the way he came with full sirens on; blue flights flashing and DC Griffin holding on to her seat belt like grim death.

Whilst the lads set off on their bikes with their inflammable payloads, Sasha and I gathered up the seine net, the other two Molotovs stuffed them into a carrier bag lying in the garage and then I tucked the crate with the Saxon Witch skull under my arm and we set off for the beach hand in hand. For the entire world we looked just like two lovers heading off to the beach for an afternoons sunbathing and necking. It was a gorgeous afternoon; in the distance I could hear the gulls and an ice cream van's jingle, and the sounds of children paying on the greensward; the tide was turning as we reached the jetty and made our way to the end. I looked at my watch, it was 12.45 pm, we didn't have long, we had to get the beast down here by 1 pm at the latest otherwise the tide would be too far in and it could escape under the water and continue to wreak havoc. I handed the seine net to Sasha with the two Molotovs and lifted the skull gingerly from the case.

"I may have to go down to the entrance to the storm drain, whatever the pull this thing has it needs to start working very soon."

Sasha looked very concerned but I scrambled down the seaweed covered jetty taking care not to damage the skull. I stood at the entrance to the storm drain and peered inside. It stank of putrefaction and dampness, the darkness stretched before me but I was determined, a cold fury had engulfed me. I almost felt like a Viking berserker, I knew this aberration had to end today.

"Don't go any further Sam," Sasha pleaded with me but I knew we had to get the Saxon Witch's skull further inside the labyrinth, so with a deep breath I started making my way towards the creature's lair. The tunnel was low but not so low I had to go on hands and knees, it was just an uncomfortable stooping position. My feet splashed in the fresh water run-off at the base of the tunnel, even though we had had no rain for weeks there was still water in the drain, and my footsteps echoed all around. I passed a few turn offs but kept heading northwards in a straight line. Every so often I'd stop and look back to make sure I could see the round circle that marked the entrance and my eventual exit. The circle of light grew pitifully small as I made my way further and further into the storm drain.

Suddenly I stopped, I felt certain I could smell smoke and then in the distance I caught a glimmer of fire. My heart nearly stopped as my eyes adjusting to the gloom ahead of me caught a glimpse of something dark moving towards me its silhouette caught by the writhing flickering flames it was running from. The supernatural howl spurred me to action and I turned and ran as if my life depended on it, which I was pretty sure it did.

My desperate splashing run was not pretty to watch but it seemed to be effective as the tunnel entrance loomed closer and closer. Water was splashing up all around me as I ran. Then another howl alerted me to the fact that the creature was close, extraordinarily close, it was impossible but I swear that I felt its hot breath behind me but then I did feel a long raking slash open my T-shirt from neck to waist and the hot sharp searing pain of a deep cut to my back, with one final burst I made the tunnel exit and as the creature pounced Sasha dropped the net on it from above. I rolled away on the sandy beach to the left, panting with fear and exhaustion. I could feel the sticky wet blood running down my back. Sasha screamed and pointed at the creature rolling around in the nylon net. It was howling and screaming and with supernatural strength seemed to be tearing its way of out the nylon net.

I got to my feet and ran to the jetty. Puffing and panting with terror and exhaustion I passed Sasha the Saxon Witch's skull and clambered back up the wooden framework, we were about ten feet above the creature. I looked around for the Molotovs and then patted my pockets for the matches. I pulled out a soggy box of safety matches, so wet the striking surface was peeling from the box. I looked at Sasha and she looked at me, I reckoned we had seconds left to live at that point, I held her hand. The creatures howling had reached a crescendo as it realised it was nearly free then I happened to look down and saw a trickle of burning fuel tumble from the storm drain. Soon a steady stream of burning petrol had puddled around the beast. The nylon netting melted and popped and sizzled, the howling reached an insane level as the creature began to burn within its nylon netted cage. The stench of burning flesh was disgusting and a cloud of black smoke billowed from the corpse rising into the still summer's air looking for all the world like a massive exclamation mark.

Eventually the thing stopped moving, the fires continued unabated. Sasha and I stood there hand in hand. We didn't hear the three lads as they dropped their bikes at the top of the beach and join us at the end of the jetty. The five of us just stood there as one. We didn't hear the sirens and the screeching police cars as we just stood and watched the thing on the beach burn away to a crisp.

I did feel a heavy hand on my shoulder and Penrose in his best Dixon of Dock Green voice say: "Hello, hello, what's going on here then lad?"

But by then it was all over.

They shoved us all in the back of the police cars and drove us all the way to Hove to make statements.

The sign on the desk read: West Sussex Police Headquarters Press Conference.

"Ladies and gentlemen," the buzz of conversation in the hall subsided as the speaker stood to address the audience, all you could hear were the pens of the ranks of journalists scribbling in their short hand notebooks, "let me introduce myself. I am Superintendent Cameron McDonald and I am here this afternoon to explain the goings on in Goring that some of you," he glowered at the assembled press corps, "seem to have rather sensationally and luridly described as the Goring Sea Monster Murders. I am going to make a statement and then I will be taking one or two questions. This morning an accidental release of flammable liquid into the storm drain system caused an inferno that led to the death of an itinerant. That unidentified itinerant we believe has been responsible for a number of murders in and around Goring beach. Following an exhaustive and difficult search of the storm drain system officers have this afternoon found the badly mutilated and burnt corpses of Charles Herbert and Andrew Newcombe, their next of kin have been informed. West Sussex Police are not currently looking for anyone else with regard to these murders and as to the release of the flammable liquids no charges are being considered."

On the stage sitting next to McDonald, Penrose caught my eye and winked and smiled.

A forest of hands shot up. McDonald pointed at one of them.

"What about the students on the beach last night? They claim a sea monster tried to attack them?" he shouted from the floor.

"Probably more to do with mass hysteria and the industrial quantities of alcohol and drugs that were being consumed," McDonald shouted back and the place dissolved into uproar.

After my wound had been dressed and treated they took us all back home. Sasha and I sat in the back of the Triumph holding hands as Penrose and Griffin drove us home. They dropped Sasha off first and after speaking for a long time to her parents they came back to the car and took me home too.

Mum was an emotional wreck, she didn't know whether to cry with joy or shout at me for being so stupid, and she was also grieving for Dad and the lost baby. A Policewoman was with her and eventually she calmed down and listed to Penrose and DC Griffin explain the whole fantastic story. Then my nan turned up and in her no nonsense fashion she ran my mum a hot bath and made her a strong cup of tea with a huge glug of Teachers whisky in it. I reckon I got to bed sometime after midnight and I fell asleep listening to Mum still sniffling in her bedroom.

Chapter 5: 2015

The rest of that summer is a vague and not entirely pleasant memory, the gash on my back festered and went septic. I spent a lot of time being pumped with anti-biotics and being kept inside by Mum. Sasha and the lads came around and we listened to music and chilled.

Mr Wetherby was right about Rick; the fags eventually did for him. He died three years ago of the big C. He achieved his ambition though and played sessions for some of the great bands in the late 80s and 90s.

GG has now got Type 2 Diabetes and is in a wheelchair after having a leg amputated, I still see him from time to time.

Sasha and I drifted apart after I went to University, she married a stockbroker and they've a huge house on the Downs overlooking Goring, she still looks amazing but I have a feeling there's been some work done somewhere.

Sean, I really don't know what happened to Sean, he moved away for work and somehow we never kept in touch. He never really forgave me for stealing Sasha from under his nose.

Me? Well I now work at the school I went to in 1974 and every day I go in the staffroom and see the staff photo with Mr Wetherby and Francoise on the wall by the notice-board and I remember the summer of 1974 . . . the season in the sun.

Nineteen Nuns on the Number 15 Bus: The Southend Zombie Apocalypse

Chapter 1: The Morning After the Night Before
. . .

Like all writers I have taken some liberties with some of the structures mentioned. Southend Pier does not have a slipway at the pier head and Traitor's Gate is not currently accessible from the River Thames, but apart

,m that I have tried to be faithful to the geography of the Thames Estuary

Any resemblance to real persons, living or dead, is purely coincidental.

Nineteen Nuns on the Number 15 Bus: The Southend Zombie Apocalypse

Chapter 1: The Morning After the Night Before . . .

I'd just left my flat, it was just after 6 a.m. and I was due to meet my boss at 7 a.m., we always met up on Monday morning to review the weekend's events to see if anyone needed one of my "special" visits. I was dressed in my Monday specials: motorcycle boots, black jeans, white shirt and a long black coat. I know you're thinking "that's a bit Matrix", well you'd be right; in my line of work impression is a big thing. I am 5ft 11" but in those boots I am over 6 foot and I look menacing. It was the dog days of October, if there is such a thing, quite nice during the day but chilly in the evening. Winter is coming, I smiled.

Some instinct told me that something was really wrong when I saw the shoes in the phone box. That looks bloody weird, I thought, and then I looked closer and realised that the red stuff spattered around the box wasn't paint it was blood, lots and lots of it . . . and the shoes still had feet in them, you could just see the bones sticking out of the red gloop. It put me off the granola bar that I'd been munching on in lieu of breakfast. It was quiet too, really quiet. I could also smell smoke, not just smell it, see it. There was haze in the air and ash seemed to be drifting about like the first snowflakes on a winter's morning. It all felt distinctly otherworldly. The local newsagent was closed but the board for the *Evening Echo* for Saturday said something about "BLOODY RIOTS IN LONDON", so what I thought, nothing new there.

My weekend had been my own. I'd been away . . . well, when I say away I was on a *Game of Thrones* binge, Friday evening right through to Sunday night, in the flat on my Jack Jones. A fridge full of beer, some Jack

Daniels and coke and a host of frozen pizzas. No phones, no news, just me and kind good natured people of Westeros! My flat's a two bed-roomed affair with "glimpses of the estuary" according to the estate agent, which means if I stand on a chair and lean right out of the window I might see the sea on a good day. *Game of Thrones* the whole dammed series in one long binge and by god it was good.

As usual I'd heard a few sirens during the night but living alone I thought nothing of it. After all this was Southend, if you don't know Southend it's a "seaside" resort on the Thames Estuary about 40 miles from London, it owes its existence to the railways and the insatiable desire for working class families from London to get to the beach and paddle in the sea. Its heyday was in the 1900s and it did go downhill quite fast but it's picked up a bit since then. Kiss me quick hats, fish and chips, slot machines, miles of mud at low water, the longest pier in the world and arcades—that's Southend.

I'd heard the news on Friday afternoon about the plane from Kabul and the weird case of the man who went berserk and started biting the cabin crew and passengers, but when it landed safely at Heathrow it went out of my mind. I was too busy looking forward to finding out how Ned Stark saved Westeros, so you can imagine the ending of season one was a right shock . . . believe me, and as for the Red Wedding. In my line of work you don't have friends and you certainly don't have girlfriends, if you do they get hurt by bad people trying to get at you. I'd not had a phone call, a text or even looked at my mobile all weekend. If the boss wanted me he'd call, I don't have many people in my "contact" list.

I suppose I ought to introduce myself, Tim Burton, yea I know it's funny but that's really my name. I am an enforcer for Miles Penrose, and you don't know him. In fact, no one really knows him but if you are dealing drugs or running whores in Southend then you know of him and you probably wish you didn't. Miles controls Southend's nightlife, he runs casinos, he runs night clubs and anything that is illegal he runs as well. If you aren't paying dues to Miles you should be, and if you try to dodge it—you might meet me. I am not your typical Essex hard man though, not at all. I have no tattoos, I have hair and I don't have any dogs. To be honest I hate dogs, it seems around here every scrote seems to think it's a badge of honour having some poor mutt on a lead slathering and growling away. Any time I've had to deal with one of these morons the dog just never bothers me, they almost seem a bit scared of me.

I actually was pretty good at school, though obviously a bit of a loner, it's not that I don't like people but people tend to avoid me. I am a bit odd, I don't like odd numbers for a start and my kitchen cupboards are a wonder. All the labels of the tins face outwards and they are arranged by best before or sell by date.

Anyway, I left school with a good set of grades, and went to Sixth Form, got some reasonable A levels and started University. To be honest it was a drag, I got into a bit of bother so I jacked it in and came back to Southend. I worked a few clubs mainly as a bouncer, where I learnt to handle myself, and when Miles asked if I could do some special work for him I jumped at the chance. It mainly involved putting the frighteners on a few local dealers who thought they could subvert the Penrose system. After a visit from me and a trip to casualty it soon became clear that Miles was the man in charge. That meant I had to watch my back, a lot! I rarely carry a gun unless I need to but I always have one or two little surprises available. Nothing that would alert the old bill but it's surprising how much damage a Swiss Army knife can do at close quarters.

The thing is though I am a fair bit brighter than the muscle heads and psychos employed by most of the dealers and pimps in the town. They respect me and they also fear my attention to detail and my cold look. They never know what I am thinking and that's what scares them the most. I might invite them for a drink in the local boozer or break their fingers one by one. I have to admit here that I am not a violent man, but if Miles gives me a job to do, it gets done. One way or the other. I think that's just part of my OCD but I won't give up until I've achieved what he asks me. Did I mention the fact that I am just a bit geeky as well? DC Comics, Marvel, *Doctor Who* I love 'em all. *Spiderman* is probably my favourite though, a dark superhero with everyday hang ups . . . I wonder why?

That's when the 6.07 a.m. bus came around the corner, fast, really fast. It was the Number 15, that upset me a bit, on the way to Hamlet Court Road and even as it slewed around the corner I could see the nuns. You don't see many nuns in Southend, unless you get a hen-do on the sea front from London, getting pissed and flashing their bits and L-plates at passers-by. These though were the real McCoy, wimples and all, nine rows of nuns sitting side by side facing me and one sitting forlornly at the front on her own. Nineteen of them in all and that upset me even more. I smiled at the one sitting alone, but you couldn't mistake the panic in her eyes as the driver overcooked the corner. The wheels whined in protest and then the front wheels hit the kerb with an almighty racket then it simply paused and then gracefully toppled over.

Now I am used to bit of carnage but that shocked even me, the noise of the crash was horrendous, there was glass everywhere and people screaming in agony. Then I looked at the driver again and realised that someone, or something was attacking him. His eyes met mine, I don't think I've ever seen someone so scared and believe me I've seen a fair few scared people. Then his attacker bit his throat and his eyes just rolled over. I knew he was dead. His attacker turned to the inside of the bus and the screaming intensified. I did think about doing the Peter Parker bit but to be frank I was more than a bit freaked out. What the hell was going on here?

So I legged it, double quick, and headed for Miles Penrose's penthouse which unsurprisingly was on the seafront, in a prime location, one of those gaffes that just screams money, big money. Hamlet Court Road was a mess. I can't think how I hadn't noticed it before. Shop windows broken, glass strewn across the road, bodies lying in and out of doorways and some of the bodies were being fed on by people. I kept to the middle of the road, legs pumping like pistons and breathing like a 40-a-day addict I sped across the railway bridge and headed down one of the side streets onto the esplanade. The esplanade was deserted, cars left abandoned in all sorts of positions across the road. It looked apocalyptic and when I turned to the west the sky was hideous. In the direction of London all you could see was smoke and flames, Hadleigh Castle was silhouetted against the blood red sky, at any other time I'd have stopped and taken a picture but my sudden arrival on the esplanade had disturbed a group of people who appeared to be feeding on the corpse of a young man. Hands on my knees trying to get my breath back I clocked that one by one they stopped feeding and fixed their red bloodshot eyes in my direction, sniffed the air and growled like wild animals. I suddenly felt very, very aware that I might soon become as dead as the bus driver and the nuns on the bus.

I ran again, the one thing I had noticed was that whatever was feeding off the dead, they couldn't move that fast. Jerky steps at best, but if you got cornered they looked pretty mean. I still could see that look on the bus driver's face trapped in his cab, screaming in pain. I reckon I'd covered about two miles that morning already and it wasn't even 7 a.m. The apartment block wasn't far now and I had keys for the entrance, there were thirteen walkers (another odd number—today was really bloody awful) behind me now lurching towards the block. I quickly opened the doors and went into the lobby. Aluminium, steel and glass, very nice, it must have cost a pretty penny. I reckon Miles paid more in maintenance costs than I did on my mortgage every month! The doors closed behind me and I could see the lurching walkers about 50 yards away. I needed to get out of the lobby, I wasn't convinced that those elegant glass doors would stand up to any form of direct or sustained assault. The button on the lift lit, thank goodness for that with all the chaos outside I was pleased that the electricity supply was still working though I had serious doubts as to how long it would last. The lift arrived as the zombies did and as I stepped through the elevator doors the mob crashed against the glass doors. It held and as the lift doors closed I could see the raging mob outside. Furious faces snarling, baying, spitting and clawing at the glass. I wouldn't want to have mixed it with that lot.

Miles had a penthouse, really stunning place. Views right over the estuary to Kent. Miles was bit of a film buff and he and I would chat about films a lot. He even collected film memorabilia and spent a fortune on eBay buying movie artwork and the like. I opened the door gingerly to a sight that quite frankly I couldn't believe. Miles completely naked and very pale was wedged into his chair at his huge oak desk. Miles was clinically obese, he must have weighed in excess of twenty stone, and when I mean wedged I mean wedged. I gasped as I noticed his hands; they were nailed to the table. Six inch nails driven through the green leather right through the oak below. His ear was bitten off and blood had oozed out forming a crust on his shoulder, to me he appeared stone cold dead. I stepped through the door and froze.

I felt rather than heard someone else in the flat. It's a sixth sense that goes with my OCD and it's been very useful more than once. I moved slowly into the room, the light was stunning, sunrise lit the room illuminating the original movie artwork on the walls and huge white leather sofa and the 52" TV and sound system in the corner. The mammoth array of bookcases filled with rare 1st editions, he even had a signed set of *The Lord of the Rings* trilogy in dust wrappers, as well as H. P. Lovecraft's legendary *The Outsider* and then there were models of the Tardis, the Millennium Falcon and Nostromo on display. My eyes kept drifting back to Miles, sitting there like a vast Buddha.

I heard a noise from the kitchen and I inched over to the door which was slightly ajar. I grabbed the first heavy thing I could. It was an Oscar that Miles had purchased on eBay from a dodgy dealer in the States. It weighed a fair bit and I knew that if it connected with a cranium it could do a lot of damage.

The door swung open and coming out with a plate on which stood two pieces of toast was the most gorgeous human being I'd ever seen.

"You must be Tim," she said, her voice was slightly accented, Eastern European I guessed. Dark hair, green eyes, tight blue jeans and a figure to die for. I reckoned she was about five foot three and wearing a simple white blouse. A vision of loveliness on what had been so far a pretty damn ugly day . . . and then I saw the hammer in her other hand.

Chapter 2: How to Deal with Demanding Management

"Okay, sweetheart," I said, "what's going on here, and just who the hell are you?"

She smiled and made her way over to the cream leather sofa facing the estuary and sat down as calm as you like and started munching the toast.

"I'm your worst nightmare," she said, flicking crumbs from her gorgeous ruby lips, "or I was," and she waved her hand to indicate the scenes of chaos outside. Somewhere in the distance I heard the sound of a siren then a loud crump and then the siren stopped abruptly.

"Oh, and by the way I am not your sweetheart, my name is Tania. I had a contract to fulfil. Sunday night pick up fat boy over there, take him somewhere quiet and make sure no one ever heard from him again. Then it was going to be your turn. Sadly, things went a bit pear shaped, and I never got to make the hit."

I was astonished. I slumped onto the sofa and watched her face. I am pretty good at reading faces and I could tell she wasn't lying. Those green eyes just kept looking right back at me, no way she was lying. I put the Oscar statuette down by my side.

"So what happened," I said. "Tell me everything."

"I work for Paddy Biggs," she said, and then it twigged. Paddy's a mean little bastard works out of Pitsea. He runs a two-bit operation over there that covers East Basildon. He says he's related to Ronnie but I think that's bullshit. They say you haven't lived until you'd seen the sun rise over Pitsea tip and that's even more bullshit! Miles knew of him but he hadn't really been bothered him and vice versa. "Paddy decided he'd had enough of small fry crack-heads in Pitsea and he thought it was time to move up the food chain. When he saw there were no vacancies he decided to make one. I came over from Croatia last week. The offer was substantial; I couldn't turn it down. I grew up in a tiny little village near Gašnica just by the Serbian border, my mum was a single parent and my sisters and I had it tough, I mean tough. I killed my first man when I was 12, he tried to rape my younger sister when we were collecting mushrooms in the woods, he was Serbian." She spat on the floor in disgust, "and after that people came to me to fix problems for them." I smiled as that's near enough my story, without the attempted rape I hasten to add.

Very interesting though, so that's why we'd never heard a whisper, I thought to myself, someone from Europe. Paddy played a canny game this time. I wondered how he'd got the cash together. That sort of hit was going to cost a pretty penny.

"It started so well, I made a move on Sunday in the club on the seafront." She sighed. "And then all hell broke loose. Your boss was besotted; I had him eating out of my hand in minutes. He was all over me like a rash. We'd just settled down to champagne cocktails when his bouncers ran in from outside. You could see they were terrified, a couple of them were bleeding and they were screaming about shutting the doors."

I could picture the scene especially after what I'd witnessed this morning, cowering punters and a mob of zombies at the doors.

Tania continued, "The bouncers tried, oh they tried but those beasts were too strong for them and inch by inch the doors slid open. The bouncers were getting bitten by then and I knew we had to get out of there and fast. We got behind the bar and crawled away to the delivery entrance. Luckily the Jaguar that Miles owned was parked not far away. We thought we'd got away with it and then he pressed the remote to open the doors. The beep from the remote and the flash of the lights on the car attracted the zombies, within seconds we could hear them rushing to us. I got in the passenger seat but Miles wasn't quite so fast and a zombie bit him on the head, ripped his ear right off. He got in with blood gushing everywhere; he kicked the zombie in the face and managed to lock the doors. By this time there was a pack of zombies bashing at the windows and crawling over the car. I've never seen such animal hatred. Miles got the car started and drove off, he must have flattened half a dozen of them. Wheels squealing, we made it on to the 20 mph zone." She smiled. "But we must have been doing 70 mph at least. A couple of zombies tried to stop us but they got smashed to pieces."

She stopped and I could see that the effect of narrating the tale was taking a toll on her. She might be an ice cool fixer but after last night's shocks there was vulnerability about her that I found quite touching and very attractive.

"I suppose we got back here at about 2 a.m.," she continued. "Miles was barely conscious. He was sweating profusely, he looked grey and his breathing was very shallow, he took all his clothes off and sat where you can see him. I knew full well what was going to happen. He died about 5 a.m. and then I had no choice, I couldn't leave, the zombies were everywhere outside. Then I started to think about what would happen next, the warnings were all over the TV stations before they went off air." She grimaced. "He'll turn like they all do. I searched the flat for rope but all I could find was the hammer and the nails underneath the sink."

At that moment an inhuman shriek cut through the flat and we both turned as one to see the re-incarnation of Miles Penrose. His eye's opened, red and bloodshot and he roared with anger and hunger. Flecks of spittle dropped from his mouth onto the green leather of the table below. His muscles flexed and imperceptibly the nails started lifting from the table. I was flabbergasted. The hate radiated off him in waves, he roared again and another few millimetres of nail were revealed. We didn't have long. I grabbed the Oscar and bounded over to the desk. Standing behind him I said calmly, "And the award for best zombie impersonator is . . . Miles Penrose," and I smashed the statuette as hard as I could onto his bald pate, a sickening crunch, a roar of anger, then another crunch as I hit him again and then silence.

"I don't think anyone's ever used an Oscar for killing a zombie before." I grinned.

We both jumped as the door buzzer from the lobby went off, cutting through the silence like a gunshot. "What the hell," I snarled. The video entry phone was by the front door. I looked at the video and the lobby was full of snarling growling zombies. I reckon they must have pushed it by accident.

"Well, there's no way out by the front door," I said.

"So what do we do now?" Tania's voice sounded a bit subdued. I think she realised that we really were in a jam. The prospect of being a walking smorgasbord for a zombie was distinctly unappealing to me too.

"Well, we can't stay here," I said. I walked over to the window, the view never failed to impress me. The whole estuary looked beautiful, the flags blowing stiffly by the Casino towards the green Kent shore in the distance and the long grey strip that was Southend Pier cutting a mile and a bit into the sea. I smiled. "Tania," I said, "I think I've got somewhere we could go that could be safe."

Chapter 3: How to Get Out of a Tricky Situation (Part One)

I sat down again and Tania asked me if I wanted a cup of tea. I tried to put on the TV but all I got was static. I then checked my phone. No network. I really was bemused about this catastrophic turn of events. When Tania came back I gestured for her to sit and asked her what had been going on since Friday afternoon. I explained about the GoT binge-a-thon. She smiled, and even though I thought she looked gorgeous anyway, when she smiled the whole atmosphere in the room changed for the better.

"So," she said, "did you hear about the Kabul flight that landed at Heathrow?" I nodded, I was going to remind her that you should never start a sentence with "So" but I thought better of it.

"Well that's where it started and it spread, did it spread. They shut Heathrow immediately but it was too late. The zombies spread, the

M25 turned into a killing field as massive traffic jams formed and zombies feasted on the living commuters. The Friday night rush hour turned into an extended lunch hour for the zombies. During Saturday things just got worse. Planes were landing all over Europe carrying the zombie virus and zombies were causing mayhem. Glasgow, Edinburgh, Manchester, Liverpool all succumbed. The news pictures were awful. We thought they'd contained it within the M25 cordon but sometime on Sunday the zombies broke out. The virus is spread by bites, and if bitten you die and . . ." She nodded in the direction of Miles.

"You come back." I finished her sentence. She shuddered.

"Okay," I said, "we've got work to do." I grabbed her hand, she instinctively drew back but I kept hold of it. "Look," I said. "It's just you and me now, if we work together we live, if we don't, we die. I know that you'd have killed me without a second thought but this whole world's gone screwball. I reckon we've one chance to get out of here to a place of some safety. Are you with me?" I squeezed her hand in reassurance.

She smiled and nodded her assent.

"Right," I said vehemently, "let's get started. Have you any weapons?"

She shook her head; her hair was really gorgeous. I think I might have said that already. "I was going to deal with you both." She smiled. "With this." With a flourish she produced a vial of clear liquid from inside her blouse. I blushed as I realised where it must have been stored.

"Not sure how effective that will be against zombies," I said. "There's my motorbike in the basement garage, we need to get down there as soon as. We will need some gear though, go and check the kitchen, we will need matches and some knives."

I went out into the hall, checking the peep hole for any signs of lurker activity. It wouldn't be long before the building was overrun. All clear, so I cracked the door open and checked again. My nerves were screaming. I went over to the fire exit and prised open the case containing the extinguisher and the fire axe. I slipped the axe out and hefted it from hand to hand. It felt good. I called the lift and stood beside it axe raised. It arrived with a ping and the doors opened to reveal . . . an empty lift. I smashed the control panel with the axe and wedged the fire extinguisher in the doorway to prevent it from being used. The last thing I wanted was a lift full of zombies opening on us at an inopportune moment.

Tania appeared with an array of kitchen knives and matches. "See if you can find a holdall or a rucksack," I said and she disappeared back into the apartment, returning a few minutes later with a Virgin gym rucksack. That surprised me, I hadn't thought of Miles as a gym bunny. Oh well, maybe I didn't know him as well as I thought.

"I've put together a few other items we might need," she said as she swung the bag onto her shoulders securing the straps.

Together we stood before the fire exit, I cracked the bars and we both breathed in as I eased the doors open. Not a sound came up the stairway so we both scrambled through the doors and shut them behind us. "So far, so good," I whispered.

The climb down to the basement was stressful to say the least. The closer we got to the ground floor the greater the noise of the baying pack of zombies in the lobby became. My heart was pounding especially when we crept past the lobby fire escape door one of them smashed against it with full force. The door flexed but nothing else. I put my fingers to my lips and we crept past. The door came under renewed attack; the bastards could smell us! I grabbed Tania's hand and we ran down the final flight of steps.

The basement garage was dimly lit; I could see my bike with the tarpaulin over it next to Mile's motor. He was a Jaguar man, an F-Type coupe, bright red, 12,000 miles on the clock and it looked gorgeous, apart from the blood stains across the hood and the dents in the windscreen and the front grille. "It had a few bumps last night." Tania giggled.

We made our way across the garage, I lifted the boot and got two jerry cans of petrol out. Swiftly I pulled the tarpaulin off the bike and Tania gasped. It's my pride and joy, it's the olive green Triumph Bonneville T100 Steve McQueen Special Edition. It's a twin 865cc engine and gives me 67hp at 43 miles per gallon, if you've seen *The Great Escape*, and let's face it, who hasn't, then you'll know it. It's the one Steve McQueen rides and nearly succeeds in jumping the fences on the border. Mine has had some conversions, for a start it's got a double seat, some panniers and a few other modifications. I stashed the jerry cans safely in the panniers and we got ready to leave.

Just then we heard the lobby fire exit door explode inwards with a crash and with an exultant howl the mob began to descend towards us.

"Hurry," I yelled, and I jumped on the kick start, it started with a meaty roar and as the zombies descended into the lobby Tania clambered aboard. I knocked it into gear and cruised up the ramp into the warm October sunshine and headed east towards the pier. A single zombie emerged from the bushes at the top of the ramp; my motorcycle boot smashed his head in as I accelerated away.

Chapter 4: How to Get Out of a Tricky Situation (Part Two)

Driving along Southend seafront was a pleasure at the best of times. With Tania behind me, my coat billowing out behind and not another car on the move it was weirdly pleasurable. We motored past the Arches cafes, past the Cliffs Pavilion perched precariously on the edge of the cliffs, past the Casino with its flags still flying and headed towards the pier. I deftly manoeuvred the bike between the pile ups and abandoned vehicles and we made slow but steady progress. We saw zombies everywhere and precious few live people but we did see plenty of dead ones. Most of the zombies stopped their grisly feasting and began following the noise of the bike. It is pretty distinctive. After we went past Adventure Island, the old amusement park, I headed towards the pier entrance and bumped the Triumph up the kerb. Behind us the magnificent façade of the Park Inn gleamed white in the mid-morning sunshine. At the top of Pier Hill, a huge group of zombies who'd gathered at the end of the High Street watched us enter the gloom and as one started to track their way towards us.

The gate was locked with a chain and a padlock, I jumped off and after a couple of lusty blows the padlock shattered and we drove through as the baying mob of zombies appeared out of the gloom behind us. The pier is one point "who gives a toss" miles long and we got to the end in under a minute. I roared down the pier, wind in my face and the bike wheels vibrating as they hit the deck boards, weaving between the various shelters. I could see the zombies behind us and I reckoned we had at best twenty minutes.

Tania got off the bike and I give her the jerry cans from the panniers and her instructions. "Go about ten metres towards the shore and pour the petrol across the boards. Don't waste it, make sure the boards are soaked and when you are ready light the fuel, go right across the pier," I said. "We must destroy these deck boards."

In the meantime, I got to work with the axe. I had to make a fire break otherwise Tania and I would simply get burned to death or become a zombie's pepperoni. I smashed the axe down, splitting the deck boards and creating a hole. I looked down into the grey, cold waters and contemplated them as a preferable alternative to being eaten alive. There was a whoosh as Tania lit the fire and the zombies roared as one at the flames ahead of them. They still hadn't got half way down the pier but as I struggled like a mad-man to destroy something that had existed for a nearly two centuries I wondered whether our events might all be in vain. Splintered boards lay around me and Tania joined me as she ran back from the fire. Soon we had a gap approaching two feet the width of the pier as the zombies got closer so did the fire get to our makeshift break. My hands were bleeding and Tania's nails were wrecked but as the first of the zombies approached the fire damaged area I wasn't sure that we'd done enough.

The as the mob hit the burnt area the smouldering timbers collapsed with their weight and wave after wave of zombies fell into the icy Thames waters beneath. The fire still burned towards us, driven by the northerly wind I'd noticed from Miles' apartment and we soon felt the heat on our faces. The zombies though kept coming, pushed on by the bloodlust of those behind they just kept on coming and kept on falling. Slowly the fire began to dwindle; the flames reached our rather pitiful fire break, faltered and died. One or two sparks floated across the gap but we easily dealt with those with our feet. Between us and the zombies was a clear space of about ten metres. The odd thin metal pole ran from where we were to the zombie's side but there was no way any human let alone a zombie could walk along it. The waters boiled with zombies scrabbling over each other to try and escape their watery fate, the Thames current was strong and pretty soon the majority were swept out towards Shoebury, Foulness and the grey forbidding North Sea beyond.

The remaining zombies, nonplussed at the turn of events began to realise that there was no way they could get to us and slowly they turned and shuffled back to the land in search of easier prey. Tania turned to me and hugged me tight. "Bloody hell," she said, "that was close." Her brown hair was lightly singed from the petrol but she still looked beautiful.

I turned to survey our new home. At the end of Southend Pier, there's a triangular area of decking and on it there's the RNLI lifeboat station, the Southend Pier Museum, a gift shop and a café. The deck had a docking area for boats about fifteen feet above the level of the water and dotted at regular intervals around the edge of the deck were lifebelt stations, with lifebelts that could "Only be used in the event of an emergency". You might have seen Jamie Oliver cook at the café as he did a programme on the telly, pretty dull as I recall.

"This is it Tania," I said, "our new home or it could be our last resting place." I shivered as a dark cloud drifted across the face of the sun. The café was an award winning design I remembered reading about it. It looks a bit like a grey angular shed, with its angular roof and strange geometry it wouldn't be out of place in Area 51 but to my eyes it looked wonderful.

I have to say I was starving. It seemed that most of the day I'd been running and now we had a chance to take stock I felt that I needed a cuppa and some food. We climbed the few wooden stairs leading to the door of the café. The door didn't last long when I took the axe to it and nor did the doors to the storage area. We both smiled when the doors swung open to reveal a warehouse full of food, canned meats, dried food, and other sundries, the meat locker had a stack of frozen food in it and the power was still on. Our luck had lasted all day and this was just the icing on the cake.

I grabbed some tea bags and some dried milk and went back to the café area. A dozen tables and chairs had been laid out ready for the customers who never came. I filled a kettle with water and set it to boil.

"It's going to be dried milk, I am afraid, at least until I can get a cow out here." I called to Tania, who was rummaging around in the storeroom.

"No problem," she replied and emerged carrying a bag of ingredients. "Tonight I will cook for you my special Goulash, to celebrate!" She giggled girlishly and I laughed along with her.

She got to work preparing the ingredients in the café cooking area. I made her a cup of tea, took it into the preparation area and left it by her side. She was working with fresh peppers, paprika, a tin of beef, tins of tomatoes, and other bits and pieces. I left her to it, took my tea with me and went outside for a recce.

The sun was well beyond high. It had been a very busy morning and now here we were in a place of relative safety. I felt sorry for all the people in Southend, but we'd had to save ourselves first, then if we could help others then all well and good. Looking south towards Kent the Lifeboat station was to my left, I wanted to explore that soon. I had a feeling that the lifeboat would be the best bet for any excursions we would have to make when the food got low. I wandered over to the lifeboat station, the wind was picking up and I could smell burning again coming from central Southend. I heard a faint explosion coming from Canvey way. The lifeboat station had an observation tower and I presumed some sort of radio equipment. The door had one of those long bars across it that should have been secured with a padlock at either end, it wasn't secured at all that surprised me and made me wary.

I paused at the entrance to let my eyes adjust to the gloom inside. Then, bang, it hit me like an express train. A huge zombie soaking wet, seaweed in its hair and that awful gaping maw aimed right for my neck. As I fell backwards I managed to get my hands on its throat but it needed all my strength to keep those slavering jaws at bay. Staring up at its blood crazed eyes; I really thought my time had come. After everything I'd been through today to end up as a zombie sushi was really sad.

Then the thing's head exploded with a mighty crump as a hammer came flying through the hair. Tania was standing about ten feet away her eyes staring and panic all over her face. Blood, gore and bits of bone littered the surrounding area.

"It came up the slipway," she cried. "I saw it from the kitchen window and ran as fast as I could."

I pushed the soggy corpse off me, it took some effort, I can tell you. "Well thanks," I said, "you certainly got me out of tight spot there. The slipway! Damn, how could I have been so stupid?"

Of course, they had to launch the lifeboats and in the excitement it had completely slipped my mind.

"Were there any others?" I asked.

"No, just him, it, or whatever you call it. The rest got swept away, he must have been strong enough to get round," she replied.

I got up and for the second time today, she came over and hugged me tight.

"I thought you were finished," she whispered.

"So did I," I replied. "Come on, let's get some food inside us."

I took another look inside, just in case. We needed to ensure there were no more nasty surprises like that again. The RNLI lifeboat was at the top of the slipway, a big orange beast, about 8m long with huge twin outboard motors. It looked really impressive, if only I knew anything about boats! We made our way back to the café. Tania had found a bottle of Rioja and a couple of candles. I pulled the blinds down, and we sat and talked, and drank and ate. Two people who this morning would have killed each other without blinking but who now faced a very uncertain future.

I won't bore you with the details but after dinner, we got closer, a whole lot closer, and I learnt a few very naughty Croatian words . . . and Tania learned how to speak a bit Estuary like . . . innit. Strange thing was though, later as I held her in my arms listening to the waves crashing against the piles of the pier and the raucous cries of seagulls in the distance I'd never felt so much at peace.

Chapter 5: Things Can Only get Better or so You'd Think

Tuesday started a whole lot better than Monday. I woke up before Tania, got her a cuppa, took it into her, she looked gorgeous so I kissed her on the cheek and went out. I washed and spruced up in the toilets in the café and then did a few laps around the pier head. It wasn't much but it meant that I could at least try to stay in shape. Also I very cautiously checked the slipway, easing the bar away but this time all I saw was the sea, it was high tide and the water was just a couple of metres away from the top of the slipway. The sun was shining and a few high clouds scudded across the sky, the overnight chill that meant we had to get close to each other for warmth last night had soon lifted.

"Ahoy the pier head!" A loud cry startled me. "Permission to come alongside?"

A yacht under sail was bearing down on the pier head, and the voice came from a guy at the wheel waving frantically to get my attention.

"Ahoy the . . . er . . . Argo." I just made out the name in bright blue letters on the hull. "Pull alongside and I'll throw you a rope," I replied, not even thinking if this was a good idea or not.

The mariner trimmed the sails and came alongside. This guy knew what he was doing I thought as the sleek white hull, about 9 metres long, barely kissed the fenders that lined the pier head. I threw him the rope he caught it, made fast and then nimbly skipped up the ladder to the decking.

"Hi," he said holding his hand out. "I'm . . ."

"Jason," I interrupted, "the Argo was a bit of a giveaway."

He pumped my hand vigorously, "Bloody good guess, old sport, and she's a Jeanneau Sun Odyssey, 8.8 metres of yachting heaven, if you like your boats she's a beauty." He grinned.

His voice resonated old money, good public school and city boardroom and to be honest the only person I'd ever heard say 'Old Sport" was Leonardo DiCaprio in *The Great Gatsby*. He must have been 5ft 10", flecks of grey in his dark hair, I put his age at somewhere between 35 and 40, wiry though and he looked as if he ran, a lot!

"Can I offer you some tea?" I asked politely, what I really wondered was, what the hell he was doing here. Something wasn't quite right.

"That would be grand," he replied.

"So what brings you to Southend Pier head," I asked as we made our way back to the café.

"I've been moored at St Katherine's Dock since last Wednesday. I was about to go on a cruise for a late break, the weather forecast being so good, and all. I work for a large metal brokers on Canary Wharf and I keep the boat moored so I can get to it easily. I pulled out of the main dock on Friday evening after I heard the Heathrow news and tied up in the middle of the river. It didn't sound good at all. On the BBC they said it was a bio-terrorism incident, but on Sky they said it was a mutated parasite that attacked the brain stem."

"I thought a parasite was what they called people who live in Paris," I joked.

"Yea, very funny," Jason sneered. "Anyway, there are some floating pontoons just by Tower Bridge, so I moored up there. The news just kept getting worse and worse, then, one by one the news programmes began to go off air. Even then I thought it might all blow over. Saturday morning, there was no mobile signal, no TV, no nothing, and all we could hear was gunfire, sirens, troops shouting and the inhuman baying of the zombies. Cars littered

Tower Bridge, not a person in sight just hordes of the undead scavenging among the vehicles. There were fires raging all over London so I went upstream towards the MI6 building and the Houses of Parliament. I thought if there was going to be a secure area then surely it would be around Westminster."

He paused as I opened the door and we walked in together, Tania looked astonished as I walked in with Jason.

"Tania," I said by way of introduction, "this is Jason and what a story he has to tell."

Whilst we both sat down I quickly relayed the first part of the story to Tania whilst she was making Jason a cuppa. She brought it over to the table and sat down with us, raising her eyebrows at me in a questioning way. I shrugged my shoulders, what else could I do?

Jason took a deep breath, "Westminster Bridge was a disaster area, a few small pockets of armed resistance with soldiers screaming and firing at zombies everywhere and then it happened. One of them fell from the Bridge and landed plum square on the boat, just aft of the main sail. I told her not to go near it, I told her . . ." and his voice tailed off as he began to sob uncontrollably. Tania and I looked at each other at a loss as to what to do or say . . .

"She got bitten?" I asked quietly.

"She got bitten," he repeated. "Stupid cow!" His tone changed to anger in a split second. "She never listens to anything I say, always going on and on about my faults." He'd started shouting and banging his fists on the table. "Always the bloody same, on and on about me failing her, about me not doing well enough and then the stupid bitch gets bit!"

He buried his head in his hands and I wasn't sure if he was sobbing or laughing, but I knew we had a serious problem on our hands, he was very unstable.

"Jason," Tania enquired. "Another cup of tea, perhaps with a slug of scotch. You sound like you could use it after what you've been through."

He nodded and Tania picked up his cup and returned to the counter area.

"So what happened next?" I asked as calmly as I could.

"I dealt with the bitch," he replied vehemently almost spitting the words out with anger. "I dealt with her, okay, that's it, dealt with."

Tania came over and slid the tea over towards the pitiful wreck of a man. He gulped it down thirstily eyeing us both over the top of the cup. "That's a very nice cup of tea; I love the scotch in it, thank you. You've a nice place here," he said, his voice oozed with malevolence, "a man could live here like a king for a long, long time, safe and sound on your own little man-made island. It's just the place I've been looking for a zombie proof . . ."

His voice faltered and he slumped forward, head bashing the table and spilling what remained over his tea.

"What, the hell happened there?" I was gobsmacked.

Tania smiled at me and produced another small vial of a colourless liquid from her blouse.

"Benzodiazepine is a wonderful drug; it never fails me and believe me I've had to use it a few times. Especially when mixed with a dose of alcohol. Very effective and it was what I had intended to use on you, until certain 'events' intervened." She giggled and winked at me. "He will be unconscious for a couple of hours. We need to decide what to do with him and check his boat over first. We need to find out what brought him here, I don't think it was an accident."

She went back to the counter and came back with some rope. Together we tied him to the chair and then dragged it over to the storage area; I opened the meat locker and pulled the chair in.

"He can cool off in here for a few minutes." I smiled at Tania. I grabbed my axe from beside the café counter and arm in arm we set off.

As we emerged from the café, we both drew in our breath at the chill. The clouds had rolled in over the estuary and the water was much choppier than it had been early morning, a stiff easterly wind made it feel very cold indeed. We heard the metallic "clack-clack" of the rigging hitting the main mast of the Argo as we made our way across to the edge of the decking and peered down at the boat moored below.

I motioned for Tania to stay put as I clambered down the ladder and stood on the pitching deck. The rear cockpit I stepped into was quite small, with the wheel on the left and a closed hatchway to the right. Even with the slapping of the waves and the thrumming of the rigging I could hear a distinct knocking from inside the hatch.

I moved carefully towards the hatch, axe in hand and opened it carefully, very carefully. The stench hit me at once, rotten meat and a strange acrid smell that I couldn't quite place. It reminded me of the times I had had to visit cheap peepshow strip joints when I was still working for Miles. I entered cautiously; the curtains had been pulled so it was dark and dingy inside the tiny cabin, as my eyes adjusted to the gloom I began to make out the interior design. There was a central aisle and a small table between the white sofa beds on either side, a galley to my left and what I guessed to be a toilet compartment to my right. At the end of the cabin was another hatch and it was from there that the knocking was coming from. I edged forward axe held at the ready I guessed that this was the master cabin. Slowly I pulled the door open and almost puked, the smell was ghastly, putrid stench of rotten meat and then I realised what I was looking at and I almost gagged. There on the bed tied like some perverted *Fifty Shades of Grey* tableau was a zombie spread eagled. A large female with saggy breasts and a bit of a pot belly, arms and legs tied to the ends of the bed in the shape of a sickening St Andrew's cross, and completely naked. The head shrouded in a motor cycle helmet, I suppose to prevent it from biting its abuser. The body showing every sign that it had been tortured and raped, raped repeatedly. The bruising was extensive and unpleasant then I remembered what that horrible acrid smell was, semen and lots of it. There were bite marks and burns on the body too; it looked like old Jason had had himself a bit of a sadistic snuff movie zombie party on the way down the river.

Sick bastard, I thought, *really bloody sick*. The zombie was bashing its head on the headboard and struggling with the bindings, but all to no avail.

I backed out, backed out through the cabin and out into the cockpit, dragging in a lungful of clean fresh air I gestured to Tania to come down and explained briefly to her what I'd found.

"The bastard," she said echoing my own thoughts. "The filthy bastard." Her hair was blowing in the wind and I had never seen her look so angry and yet so incredibly beautiful.

"I agree," I said, "but we've got to get her out of there, this could be really useful to us and we don't know what else he has inside that may give us a clue as to why he's here. That thing could get loose at any time."

"So how do we get her out?" enquired Tania.

"I've an idea," I said and explained to Tania what we needed to do.

I made my way back in with a coil of rope that was lying in the cockpit leaving Tania on the deck next to the yard arm, I left the axe on the deck next to the cockpit, if all else failed Tania might have to use it on me! I edged my way through the cabin and back in to the bedroom. The stench was just as bad and I was breathing through my mouth as much as possible. I had to work out a way of doing this without leaving me in a small confined space with a raging zombie, helmet or not, she could still tear me from limb to limb if she got hold of me. If I cut the arms free then she could reach for me and if I cut the legs free then she could kick me and incapacitate me either way I was a dead man and she'd simply feed herself by ripping me to pieces and feeding herself through the motorcycle helmet visor at her leisure.

I got some rope around her legs in a noose and drew them together, in a flash I cut the restraining cords and pulled the noose tight, her legs came together. I took the rope to one side and secured it to the bed again. The beast was roaring with anger and whilst the ropes were holding I had no idea if they would continue to do so for much longer. "So far, so good." I smiled and did the same manoeuvre with her arms as with her legs. At that moment I had a very angry hog-tied zombie who wanted to kill me and eat me. I cut the rope securing her legs and as she rose to her feet I backtracked through the cabin as she came charging after me. I almost stumbled at the hatch but made it out into the cockpit and with a roar of anger the creature burst out from below, I crouched down and as the zombie reared over me Tania swung the yard arm with all her might. It hit the poor tortured beast between the neck and the helmet I heard the crack of her neck as she cannoned from the cockpit and hit the water with an almighty splash. She sank from sight within seconds.

"Wow," I said, "that was close."

Now we had got rid of the main problem, we took stock. Back in the cabin in a box in the toilet compartment I found two Glock 17 semi-automatic pistols, which astounded me as they are standard issue for UK police forces and MI6. The other thing I was even more surprised at was these had been modified to single shot rather than automatic fire which suggested that Jason is or had been a spook. Along with the pistols there were a couple of boxes of grenades, and underneath the small sink in the galley area two Remington 870 shotguns with enough ammunition to start a small war, and most surprisingly of all an Iridium satellite phone. Another eye wateringly expensive piece of kit, I'd seen them for sale on eBay for just under a grand.

Tania found a flare gun, and a wedding picture of Jason and a woman, a skinny shrew like woman who didn't resemble the body on the bed one bit. I was just about to leave the cabin and go back to the pier head when my eyes caught sight of an envelope protruding from under one of the cushions on the seats in the cabin. My eyes popped when I saw "MI6—for your eyes only" on the cover. I showed it to Tania. "So what the hell is Jason doing here in Southend?" She screwed her eyes up in puzzlement.

It was time to find out.

Chapter 6: Problems, Problems, Problems

We both were chilled to the marrow by the time we got back to the café. I made a decision to explore thoroughly the lifeboat station later for some big Sowester coats, it was only October and if we had to overwinter here I knew it was going to be really tough, especially if the electricity was to fail, which I reasoned it was bound to sooner rather than later. We put the arms cache behind the counter and armed with the Glock I opened the meat store and dragged a semi-conscious Jason back into the warmth.

"Now you miserable sad sadistic little bastard, we want some answers," I snarled. "And if we don't get them, then this little lady is going to have a bit of feminist revenge for what you did to that poor unfortunate on your boat."

He looked stunned. "You've been on my boat," he asked. "What did you do to her?"

"It's not what I did Jason," I whispered. "It's what this one is going to do to you," I nodded at Tania, "unless you start telling us the truth." I waved one of the Glocks in his face. "And for starters what's a city trader doing with a Glock 17 and a small arsenal of weaponry and who the hell was that tied to the bed?"

His shoulders slumped and he looked at me almost mournfully. "The truth, you want the truth?" he asked. "We're all fucked. There was only ever going to be one chance and you've wrecked it, you've wrecked fucking everything!"

"Bollocks, all you've told us is a pack of lies from start to finish. Now let's have the truth, if we don't get the truth then you're going for a quick walk down the slipway to join your zombie girlfriend in Davy Jones' locker. Yo, ho, ho . . . Old sport!" I snarled in his face. "Who was the poor dead woman in the cabin; it wasn't your wife, was it?"

"Sarah Vine, my boss," he retorted. "The vilest person I've ever worked for, continually putting me down, self-opinionated, arrogant know it all. Totally bloody useless, bad tempered harridan but she knew all the right people, rumour was she even slept with someone high up in the cabinet. When it all went belly up we were sent to get the one person whom might be able to help us out of this mess."

Tania interjected, "Sent by whom?"

"MI6, we both worked for MI6, but it is my boat. I didn't lie about that. I did bring it up-river from St Katherine's Dock as I said. The mobile network was down and there was no way traffic was moving in and out of London. All the London chopper bases had been overrun by Saturday afternoon, so we were left with one hope. Sarah and I going downriver in the faint hope of getting hold of Laura Howard. She's the best parasitologist in the world, Harvard graduate probably the keenest mind on the planet and here on a visit from the US doing a lecture tour of hospitals departments. What she doesn't know about parasites isn't worth knowing. The bods in the Department of Health think the zombie is caused by a parasite in their saliva; it attacks the brain stem, so if we can kill the parasite then we've a chance. If we can't then there's no hope. Most of the country was overrun by Sunday evening. We left Saturday night and like I said, one dropped onto the boat and bit her. Stupid bitch," he snarled. "After she was bitten she kept blaming me, swearing at me, demanding to be taken back up to HQ, in the end when she went into the coma I tied her up. The helmet was something I found floating in the Thames."

"So why did you treat her like that?" Tania spat out the question. "That was just sick!"

"Revenge, old sport, simple revenge." He smiled, and Tania slapped him hard, very hard. He laughed in a mocking way but his cheek glowed red and you could see the hand mark vividly.

"She made my life a fucking misery for fifteen years," he went on. "As far as I was concerned she was dead, I made her death a misery for twenty-four hours or so, as far as I am concerned we're even now. I am not proud of it, but you have no idea what she was like."

"Laura Howard, where is she then?" I asked. To be frank I was feeling a bit calmer now. I knew we couldn't trust the bastard but at least we were on the same side . . . weren't we?

"She was lecturing at Southend University on Friday and had gone back to the Holiday Inn by the airport; she was due to return to London on Saturday. The trains were stopped early on Saturday morning in an attempt to limit the spread of the infection. We got some 3rd Regiment Army Air Corps choppers from Wattisham Airfield in Suffolk to take a gander on Saturday afternoon but the airport was a shambles. Planes littered the runway and the terminal was on fire. It appears that the virus was deliberately brought into the country from as many different locations as possible in order to maximise the impact. We think they were suicide bio-terror bombers, pre-infected then dispatched, and almost impossible to counter. That's when the decision was taken to send us down by boat in the hope of springing her and getting her back to MI6 and the science bods. She has a minder, Her Majesties Government provides them to VIPs as a matter of course and we've been in contact with him and her by that satellite phone. When I saw you on the pier head I thought we might be able to get a rescue operation mounted from here." He paused. "But then you goody two-shoes started making judgements about me and here we are—well and truly fucked."

Tania looked at me and indicated she wanted to speak in private; we left him there tied to the chair and went over to the counter.

"What do you think? Is he telling the truth?" she asked.

"I think he is, the question we have to ask ourselves, is what we do next?" I replied.

"If we help him," she whispered, "we risk everything."

"If we don't help him, we have nothing but this pier head and the prospect of starvation and probably hypothermia in a couple of months' time. To be honest I don't think we have much choice, but I wouldn't ask you to risk yourself, you stay here and look after this place. I'll take that useless tosser and be back before you know it." I nodded in Jason's direction.

"No way," she said vehemently. "I am not going to risk losing you and being on my own! We've only just found one another. In a world where we were forced to operate alone being part of a team is really nice. Besides which, we are both pretty good at doing what we do."

I smiled, there was a lot of truth in what she said, we complimented each other rather well.

We returned to Jason.

"Is she still at the Holiday Inn?" I asked Jason. "If she is, we'll go in and get her, but we do it our way, and our way alone, if you fuck with either of us you'll end up as crab meat, like your girlfriend."

"Bring me the phone and untie me and we can speak to her now," he said.

I nodded to Tania and she went and got the phone. I untied him and sat nursing the Glock as he dialled a number.

"Put it on speakerphone," said Tania. "We all need to know what we are up against."

It rang and then a disembodied voice that sounded really panicked echoed through the café.

"Hi, it's Bran, I am working security for Dr Howard, where are you? It's getting bloody messy here."

I nodded to Jason and mouthed "answer it" to him.

"Bran, it's Jason here. What's your situation? We aim to be with you later this afternoon or early evening." Jason responded brightly in an attempt to instil confidence in Bran, he did sound rattled.

"The main doors are secure, but there are about 30-40 hostiles outside the main door but they seem pretty calm at the moment. The building is secure; the bomb proof glass seems to be able to keep them at bay. There are eight of us in the first floor restaurant, we are keeping well out of sight. Dr Howard is with me and she is fine. I don't know how long we can hold out though I have limited ammunition and we really need to be out of here ASAP."

"Bran we are working on a plan we will be in touch when we are 30 minutes away, sit tight and await our call." Jason hung up.

"So, what do we do now?" He sighed. "You guys better have something sorted otherwise we are going to lose the only hope for us, and the rest of humanity!"

"Don't worry, I have a cunning plan," I said in my best Baldrick voice. Tania looked at me as if I was mad, the cultural reference lost on her completely, but Jason smiled.

"That's a start then!" he laughed.

Chapter 7: It's Show Time

"You know about boats I presume," I asked Jason and he nodded. "There's an RNLI

Atlantic 85 lifeboat downstairs, can you handle it?" He nodded again.

"That's a beauty, twin 115hp outboard motors, bloody gorgeous beast." He grinned.

"Okay there's a slipway at Shoebury by the coastguard station it's used for launching little leisure craft and those bloody annoying jet skis but we can use it, get us there at high tide and wait for us for an hour or so, we will bring them back, but be ready to leave fast as we might have company. Can you do that for us?"

"No bloody problem, old sport, but you mustn't let the tide beat you, if it goes down the slipway too much you will never get her afloat. We get there at 6 p.m. for high tide you can't be later than 7.15 p.m., if you are later than that then its mud and zombies and zombies and mud." He shivered. "I for one don't fancy that at all."

"Agreed," said Tania. "So what are we doing whilst lover boy is waiting?"

"We've got to pick up some stuff and get those poor sods out," I said grimly.

Shoebury is a small garrison town East of Southend, much of the garrison has gone now, sold to make a hefty profit for property developers who used to thrive in South East Essex. In truth there's not much there now, it's a one horse town but there is Shoebury Vehicle Hire and that's where we need to get to first. The great thing about vehicle hire joints is that the keys are always on the premises and there's the selection of vehicles that we needed to get this job done and get us all out in one piece.

Whilst we waited for the tide to rise, we ate lunch, just some baked beans on toast and got our gear ready for the sortie. Jason went to check the boat and Tania and I prepared our weaponry. Tania opted for the Glock whilst I went for the Glock/shotgun combo and a couple of grenades and the axe tucked into my belt for good measure. I thought about taking the flare gun but I slid it under the counter, you never knew when it might come in handy. I also made sure that the satellite phone stayed with me, I was sure we would be using it later. We dressed appropriately, I found some dark fisherman's sweaters in the RNLI station, the last thing we wanted to do was draw attention to ourselves. As the tide began to rise so too did the offshore wind, I was quite pleased about that as I reasoned that if those beasts hunt by smell a strong wind might be in our favour.

The beans on toast tasted good, and we followed it up with a strong cup of tea. Jason returned with a huge grin on his face.

"That's some boat," he said. "That's a helluva boat!"

Around 5.30 we made our way through the RNLI doors, Jason had the boat tied up alongside the slipway and she did look beautiful, bright orange, the wheel in the centre where the skipper could see all around him and when Jason powered her up the noise was astonishing. It oozed power and class.

"Welcome aboard." He laughed as we stepped onto the boat and took our places at the rear by the enormous outboard motors. "This won't take long."

He cast off and took the wheel, when he hit the throttle the boat surged forward, taking my breath away and we bounded over the waves towards the Coastguard Station in the distance. I held onto Tania's hand as the little world that we called our own receded into the distance, the navigation lights twinkling in the early evening gloom. The boat leapt from wave to wave and droplets of spray caught us in the face, it was exhilarating but also terrifying, this was a voyage into the unknown. The horizon behind us was crimson and seagulls soared screeching noisily overhead.

It took us about twenty minutes and as we approached the shore Jason cut the throttle and eased towards the launching ramp. He nudged the boat onto the ramp and indicated that this was our stop.

"Mind the gap," he joked as we gingerly leapt from the bow and found ourselves on dry land. "Remember, tide and time wait for no man."

"We will see you sooner rather than later." I sounded brave but actually I was pretty concerned, we had no idea what awaited us onshore, no idea at all. Jason cut the engine completely and it was at that point we realised, the enormity of the situation, the only sounds we could hear were the waves and the gulls, no cars, no buses, no people. We felt like the last people on Earth at that point.

Tania and I took off at an easy trot jogging up the ramp and down into the small car park before heading north from the beach towards Shoebury High Street, there wasn't a soul about and I reckon we got to the vehicle hire centre in fifteen minutes or so. The wire mesh fence had a double gate that was locked with a hefty padlock, but it took just one blow with the fire axe and we were inside. There were about twenty vehicles in the compound: small vans, transits and the ones we were after. We moved cautiously, even though we were armed I didn't want to make any unnecessary noise. There was a small brick building in the centre of the compound and once again the fire axe did the job for us. The office smelled of sweat, coffee and diesel but no rotting flesh, and the keys were all lined up in a wall box.

"What we need is a Luton with a tail lift." I whispered to Tania, "Here we are," and I lifted the key from the board. Just then an almighty screeching tore through the air. The silence of the night ripped apart by the alarm!

"Bollocks, the place is alarmed, quickly we need to move," I shouted. No need for subterfuge now, we had to find the van and move fast otherwise the place would be crawling with the undead in minutes. Frantically we left the office and scanned the yard for the van, luckily there were only a handful of Lutons in the yard. I saw ours straight away and ran towards it. Tania made to move towards it but was stopped as a pitiful zombie that had been lying by the side of the door grabbed her leg; the thing had no legs and flapped frantically at her trying to get its jaws in a position to take a bite. I was still holding the axe and with a single sweep severed the hand from the arm, without any other thought I grabbed her arm and pulled her with me. The keys fitted but it seemed to take an age to get the door open, finally I unlocked it and we jumped inside just as two zombies hit the front of the van at full pelt and started banging on the windscreen.

"Come on, let's go!" Tania screamed as I fumbled under the steering column. Finally, with a sigh of relief I found the ignition and got the thing started. Slamming it into first gear and then reverse dislodged the zombies from the screen and I then made for the gates which we had unlocked. There were a handful of the undead at the gate and I smashed through them and headed northwards along the High Street. There was blood and gore and other crap all over the screen so I used the washer and the wiper. As we headed over the railway line gradually the gore disappeared and we continued past the Asda superstore and headed towards Southend Airport and our destiny.

The sky was still lit by the falling sun but the red sky was fading rapidly as we turned westwards, a few vehicles littered the carriageway but we made steady progress. I had no lights on but it was pretty easy, I didn't want to give our position away any more than I needed to. I turned to Tania and outlined the plan, she listened intently and when we got about five minutes away I stopped the van and showed her the tail lift mechanism that could be operated from inside the rear storage area. I had an override in the cab, but it would be Tania's job to lower and raise the tail lift. It was really annoying that we couldn't see into the rear space but we agreed on a series of coded messages knocked on the back of the cab to tell me where we were. Then with her in the back we set off.

The Holiday Inn backs onto the airport. It's nearly brand new with a lovely roof top bar which I had frequented in my previous life, in fact one of my clients resides in its foundations, but that's another story entirely. The only access was from the main road. When we got within sight I stopped just opposite a drive-in McDonalds, chav zombies milled around inside, it would have been hard to tell the difference from live chavs unless you knew they were undead. I knocked on the wall once; this was the signal for Tania to part lower the tailgate. When that was done she knocked again. I got on the satellite phone and dialled the number.

"Are you guys ready?" I asked.

"*Ready and waiting. We are all behind the desk in reception, we sneaked down here one by one, as instructed.*"

"Okay, lets rock and roll."

I hit the lights and gunned the engine, within seconds I was bearing down on the ramshackle mob outside the glass doors at the front of the hotel. They looked at the lights transfixed like rabbits, I don't know what the collective noun is for a group of zombies, I know it's a murder of crows but this was a carnage of zombies. I must have been doing nearly thirty when we hit them; the impact was bone crunching, in more than one sense. I scattered them and then swung around so that the tail lift was facing those huge glass doors. I knocked twice and Tania lifted the sliding doors up as I reversed at speed. The tail lift hit the glass doors about two feet off the floor and they imploded with a mighty crash, broken glass littered the floor. I stopped about three foot inside the lobby as the survivors rose as one from behind the reception desk and headed for the open doors of the Luton. I saw them running towards the rear and felt the van lurch as one by one they hit the tail lift and reached safety. Tania knocked twice on the door, all aboard and door closed. What I didn't want was to accelerate and find a number of them falling out as we sped away. I hit the gas, the wheels spun and skidded as we churned up zombies then caught on the tarmac and we left the scene. The van snaked as I screamed down the road. I did think it must have been uncomfortable for my passengers but we'd just saved them from a horrible fate. All we had to do now was get down to the slipway and safety beckoned for all ten of us. For one horrid moment my old fears returned, eleven of us with Jason. . . .

The journey back was interesting, the undead had been alerted by our earlier passage through and there were more of them around than before but we swerved and dodged and got back down through the High Street without too many problems.

As we approached the launching ramp I knocked again and Tania responded. It was time to get out and onto the boat. I drove up the ramp and parked at the top . . . to see er . . . nothing! Not a boat, no Jason not a bloody thing, just a huge expanse of water with the moon shining on it and in the far distance our pier head sanctuary lit by navigation lights, it might as well have been the bloody moon! I checked my watch it wasn't even 6.45 p.m.

I leapt out of the cab and went to the rear as Tania lifted the doors.

"That bastard has stitched us up, he's gone, deserted us, marooned us on a foreign shore!" I screamed. "He's dead; he really is a dead man walking."

"Tim, calm down, you have got us out of a lot worse than this." Her calmness was astonishing, and her trust in me humbling. "There must be a way."

The other passengers stumbled out of the van one by one.

One of them grabbed my hand and shook it. "Hi, I am Bran," he said, "thanks for that, we couldn't have lasted much longer in there." Bran was about 25, fit as a fiddle obviously SAS or Marine, stood stock straight and had a handshake that would crush breeze block.

"You might not last that much longer here," I said with an apologetic air.

A tall elegant blonde woman came up to me. "Thank you," she said. "I am Dr Laura Howard; in this bag I am sure I have the answer to this epidemic." She nodded at the medical bag and laptop case she was carrying, "But I have work to do, somewhere safe if at all possible."

"We are doing our best." I shrugged. "It's just things never seem to go according to plan."

The rest introduced themselves. One was a female doctor colleague of Dr Howard, Dr January Clark, who was also carrying a medical bag, and the other five were hotel workers, two chambermaids, a barman, the receptionist and a chef. They were equally thankful but I was not sure they would thank me if they ended up as fast food for the zombie horde on our tail.

This really was a bloody hopeless situation. The zombies were following the van and would be with us soon. We had to leave the van, but what then?

There was one faint chance, there were a few yacht clubs on the way towards Southend, the posh enclave of Thorpe Bay had more than its fair share of fake commodores and weekend sailors. We might just strike lucky. I spoke calmly to the group even though my guts were churning.

"It looks like our original plan has changed, just slightly; we are going to leave the van as it's going to be a zombie hot spot in a few minutes and head along the seafront towards Southend. There's a couple of yacht clubs on the way and we are sure to find a boat to take us to the pier head, but we move silently and swiftly," I said confidently.

We set off with me at point, Bran in the middle and Tania taking up the rear. We kept low and quiet, slipping silently along the sea wall like a crocodile of kids on their way to school. I had the Glock in my hand but I was terrified of using it. It would just draw attention.

Thorpe Bay Yacht Club was no more than three-quarters of a mile from the public ramp, but when we got there all I could see were yachts and their tenders. The yachts were onshore, their sails locked away somewhere safe and out of reach, the tiny little tenders minus their outboards were of no use either and to cap it all I could hear in the distance was the braying howls of a pack of zombies searching for flesh.

Then Bran stopped and pointed silently further up the road. Then I saw it, a Land Rover Discovery with a boat on a trailer, deserted on the highway. A fishing dory on a trailer, with an outboard, this really could be what we need. Bran and I ran over to the boat, it was about twelve feet long, and I saw the fishing rods lying on the floor and a fuel can. Bran leaned in and shook the can and smiled at me as we heard fuel sloshing around it was at least half full, things were looking up at last.

We needed to drive it down to the ramp, as I opened the door a stinking putrid snarling zombie tried to bite me, its broken and torn arm hanging loosely by its side it lurched across the front seat towards me. I jumped back startled as Bran opened the passenger door and despatched it with a shot to the head.

"Thanks," I said, but the shot had been heard by many others looking for food tonight. "There's no time to drive anywhere we have to get this in the water now, the tide is ebbing, if we don't do it now it's a race across the mud flats being chased by that lot!" The braying had increased in intensity and they now sounded really too close for comfort.

Tania stood guard as Bran and I struggled with the hitch lock, suddenly it came free and I shouted for the others to help us as we manoeuvred it across the road towards the Thorpe Bay Yacht Club landing ramp. "PRIVATE PROPERTY MEMBERS ONLY" read the sign. "All property is theft," I thought and kicked it over and we wheeled the dory up the ramp and down towards the sea. The tide was ebbing though and as we let gravity carry it down to the water I wondered if we'd be able to launch the boat.

The incessant baying and roaring was really close and as we launched the boat the first of the zombies appeared at the top of the ramp silhouetted by the street lights. Tania let off a shot and it went down, a fine head shot, but others soon started to stumble over and head down towards our position. Our group of survivors had clambered aboard and it was just Bran and I still in the water. Dr Clark had found the oars and was pulling the boat steadily away from the shore. Tania was shooting over our heads and hitting targets that went down like nine pins so I beckoned for Bran to get aboard which he did, by this time the water was lapping at my waist, my feet slowly sinking into the infamous Southend mud. I reached for the two grenades at my belt, pulled both pins with my teeth and hurled them at the ravenous horde on the ramp. The shock wave was astonishing, bits of body fell like bloody confetti and for a moment I thought that my time had come but then I felt arms pulling me into the boat as Bran and Tania lifted me aboard. Bran obviously knew a bit about boats as he got the outboard started and before we knew it we were heading towards the navigation lights of the pier head. The journey back took a lot longer than the outgoing one, we had ten people on board a Dory that probably should have seated six at best. There was a lot of bailing, a lot of swearing and moaning but gradually we pulled close to the pier head. I asked Bran to cut the engine and Dr Clark rowed the boat near enough to the jetty for me to leap across. I told them to pull away from the pier until they heard from me. I had a matter of some import to attend to. . . .

As I made my way up the slipway the heavens opened and it started pouring with rain, it wasn't of biblical proportions but it wasn't far off. I still had the Glock and with it pointing downwards I slowly but surely I made my way up the ramp to the pier deck. I slid the door open, the pier deck was clear, the rain splashing off the timbers masked any noise I might have made. The lights in the café were on so I headed for it, through the gloom and the downpour.

I really had no idea what to expect but my anger was building. I knew that was a mistake, getting angry means mistakes, 'stay cool and calm and everything will be OK' had always been my mantra but he'd put Tania and everyone at risk and I was determined to get revenge.

I paused at the door and with gun in hand I kicked it open and stepped into the room, sweeping the pistol from left to right. He was there just sitting at a table with a bottle of scotch, it looked like he'd been there a fair old time; the bottle was nearly all gone. He looked up with bloodshot and bleary eyes, no shock, no surprise and simply stated.

"You . . . you got away." Then he laughed. It was all I could do not to shoot him there and then but he had some explaining to do. I moved to the table Glock held high before me, pulled a chair out and sat opposite him. The rain dripped from me and made small puddles on the floor beneath the chair. He motioned to the bottle, offering me a drink, I shook my head, and banged the table with my fist, the bottle and the glass jumped and so did he.

"Listen pal, you have no idea who I am, what I do for a living and what I will do to you unless you start telling some simple truths." The menace in my voice was palpable and for the first time he started to look a little uneasy. I grabbed his hand, splayed it on the table and smashed his little finger with the handle of the Glock. It exploded and blood spurted across the table. He howled with pain and snatched it away from my grasp.

"That's just for starters, old fucking sport." I snarled as he nursed his hand and stared at me with a certain amount of fear and pain in his eyes . . .

"Now, the truth and make it simple. I'm a simple man but I am a violent man too."

"Okay, okay, I do work for MI6 but I am a pretty low down techie. Sarah Vine is my immediate boss and when the whole thing went pear shaped it was all hands to the pump and I was called up from the 2nd floor to the 5th floor and I was volunteered to go on this suicide mission just because I had the boat. I wasn't up for it, I wasn't trained for it and when that beast fell on to the deck I was petrified. Sarah actually saved me and put herself in front of it. She managed to push it overboard whilst I was cowering in the cockpit like a baby, then she got bitten. I didn't know what to do, I did hate her though, she did used to pick on me. So then I took advantage of the situation, I was going to just keep on going having sex with a zombie until either the food ran out or we ran aground somewhere safe. When I saw your little safe haven I admit my mind was intrigued. You've got a nice little set up here and Tania . . ." He paused as I snarled and raised the Glock again. "She's lovely. I thought that maybe I could get rid of you and take over as king of Southend Pier Head. Then it all went belly up, after I dropped you of on the ramp I was by myself and then a huge mass of zombies lurched right past me on the way to Southend. There's no way we can beat them, no way at all. I was scared, terrified so I thought sod it—leave them to it. I'm off back to the ranch to have a drink or two. This is it, it's the end of the fucking world—maybe you hadn't noticed but we are extinct, it's the end of everything."

"You bastard, you left us there to die. No thought for anyone but yourself." I pistol whipped him hard across the face; his nose took the brunt of it and immediately started bleeding.

"You're a sadistic little coward, who would sacrifice everyone on a bonfire of your own vanity." I dragged him up and made my way towards the door.

"No, please," he pleaded, but I was in no mood for his drivel or his whining protestations. I dragged him through the door into the pouring rain and took him to the edge of the burnt section that Tania and I had created. I stood there with the rain pouring down and Southend seafront in the distance, the decking of the pier stretched out before me, fires on the horizon burning out of control and smoke billowing in the wind, it was an awesome apocalyptic vision.

"The tide is dropping fast," I snarled. "This is your choice, you never gave us one so I am doing you a favour, swim to shore and face the undead or swim with the tide and find somewhere else. One thing's for sure you ain't welcome here, yo fucking ho, old sport."

Without further ado I pushed him and he tumbled over the edge. I heard the scream and the splash. I turned and without a backward glance or another thought went over to the other side of the pier head and beckoned the Dory and the survivors back to the slipway. After they'd tied up and scrambled up the ladder on to the decking we all got into the café and tried to get warm and dry.

It had been a long day for us all. With wet clothes warming on electric radiators it was positively balmy in the café. Tania and I rustled up some bacon and eggs from our dwindling store of refrigerated food. I can confidently say that if you haven't had bacon and eggs in the middle of a zombie apocalypse with a few bottles of Rioja then you haven't lived my friend.

The chef's name was Steve, a Southend boy obviously liked his own food, big angelic chubby face and a figure to match, weirdly he'd been educated at my old school, he lived in a flat in Leigh not far from where Miles had his penthouse but no sea view, he promised us that he would cook tomorrow, having taken a look at the storeroom he thought he might be able to do better than bacon and eggs. One of the chambermaids was from Southend, her name was Tracy, a smashing Essex gal of about 18, strawberry blonde and a lovely dimple on her chin, and the other was a girl from Poland called Beata who might have been a year or two older, Beata had short black hair and was tall and slender. They appeared to adore Bran and they flirted with him through the evening. The receptionist, Fion, was from Chelmsford, a town about half an hour's drive from Southend, a fairly short, busty and brassy blonde in her early 50s, who obviously still looked after herself, and the barman's name was Jay another dozy Basildon lad all attitude, fake tan and estuary accent. To be honest I think that Steve was trying to flirt with Bran too but his interests lay elsewhere. Tania and I and Doctor Laura and Doctor Clark talked long into the night about zombies and parasites and death and fate and karma and Boy George and metaphysics and superheroes. I asked Dr Clark where she's learned to row like that, she said something about Yale but I forget what. I do remember starting on a third bottle of Rioja but not much more than that. I do remember the toasts from the survivors thanking us for coming to get them, I do remember getting a pleasant sloppy kiss from Fion and a couple of pecks of gratitude from Tracy and Beata, that made me feel good, but not half as good as getting into bed with Tania and cuddling her before falling into a blissful dreamless sleep.

Chapter 8: The Morning After the Night Before (Haven't We Already Done that One?)

"You bastard." I woke up to Tania moaning. "You snored all night, no more red wine for you."

Morning broke, the sun rose and so did we, fitfully and with thick heads. As the sun came up over the horizon the ten of us stirred, the party had been great but now we had to face the future. Tania, Laura, Bran, January and I sat around a table. Steve set to in the kitchen area and Tracy and Beata fussed about helping him and supplying copious amounts of tea and coffee.

"My theory," Dr Howard said, "is that this parasite is derived from a Jewel Wasp."

"A what?" said Tania.

"A Jewel Wasp, also known as an Emerald Cockroach is a remarkable creature. It lives in the tropics and it has a remarkable trick. It injects a venom into the brain of a cockroach and the cockroach loses all its powers of self-determination, it then lays its eggs in the belly of that cockroach and they hatch out in a few days' time. In effect it becomes a zombie. Somehow or other someone has managed to isolate that neuro-toxin and create a parasite that lives on a human's brain stem. It's transmitted by saliva through biting and once in the bloodstream it kills and then takes over the host. The host's sole function after that is to find another living being to transmit and spread the parasite. I have been researching just such a possibility, the CIA has scientists looking at all sorts of ways terrorism can develop and we've long been aware of the possibility of some crackpot doing exactly this. Infect your carriers load them onto planes and send them all over the world. A terrifying possibility that looks to have succeeded all too well."

"So is there a cure?" I asked, to be honest I felt a little out of my depth here.

"No, there is no cure, as such." Dr Howard continued, "But I might be able to create a serum that destroys the parasite. If we could do that then we would halt the advance, the hosts would die and not be reincarnated. I have been working on just such a serum over the past few days and I believe that Dr Clark and I have found something that just might work."

Dr Clark nodded and continued, "There's just one thing though we need some subjects to test it on."

I hesitated. "By subjects, you mean actual zombies, live ones?"

"Technically they aren't alive." Dr Clark smiled at me. "But yes we need walking dead ones."

"How many," asked Bran, obviously as alarmed as I was at the thought of capturing them, killing them no problem but capturing something whose sole purpose in life was to eat you, just didn't add up.

"We can use them one at a time, we can see if the serum works and hopefully it does then we won't need any more. There are only a handful of serums that we've perfected, if it does work then we can get in contact with the authorities and it can be mass produced. Most of the serums can be transmitted by airborne means so we could, in theory, carpet bomb a place with the serum and it would wipe out the local un-dead. Troops could then move in with aerosol sprays, a bit like pepper sprays to clear any left." Dr Howard made it all sound so simple.

"Okay, but Tania stays here, we need her to look after everyone if we don't get back." She started to protest but saw the look on my face as I shook my head. I wasn't making any concessions on that today.

I had a plan but it did involve risks. I looked around the room. The two girls were chatting to Jay and Steve was busy working behind the counter. Fion was helping Steve, it looked so normal but I knew we still had lots to do. It was easier when there were just two of us, now the group dynamic had changed enormously. The other thing, of course was that by increasing the size of the group to ten we'd just reduced drastically the amount of time we could live off of the café stores.

I rapped my spoon on the table, it went quite quickly.

"Guys, I know you've only just got to a place of relative safety." As I spoke the lights flickered but came back on again. It was a timely reminder of just how precarious our little world was. They were all looking at me intently, I was tempted to do the "Englishmen now abed will think themselves accursed they were not here" from *Henry V* but it was probably inappropriate, what with two American, a Pole and someone from Basildon who probably had no idea who "Will I am" Shakespeare was any way. "But Dr Howard and Dr Clark think they may have stumbled on something . . . the problem is they need walking, talking living dead ones to work on. Now I can't force anyone to come with me but I will ask for volunteers, I respect anyone who thinks they can't help but if you can please tell me."

Bran nodded to me and I smiled, he's already proven himself to be a go to guy in a tight situation, Beata volunteered and so did Jay—I kinda expected Jay to if one of the girls did.

"Right lads and lasses, we've got some planning to do. Let's head over to the RNLI station where we can plan in peace and get ourselves fully equipped." The rain had abated during the night and it was a chilly but calm October morning.

In the RNLI we went up to the observation room, and on a large map table I laid out our remaining weapons. We still had the Glocks, the shotguns, a box of grenades, less the two I had used last night. I still had the axe and there were also a good number of ugly looking boathooks which we'd found in the RNLI station, long wooden poles about two metres long with a metal hook at the end used for snagging lines and buoys. I thought they could come in quite useful someday. Bran had a satellite phone and so did I. I had hoped that someone might have contacted us from MI6 but they'd remained stubbornly quiet.

"I don't think we will need much weaponry so I am just intending to take the Glocks, we will need a lot of rope and something to cover the head of the zombie so it can't bite any of us. If it does we are in deep trouble, Jay and Beata can you have a look round downstairs and see if you can come up with something?"

As they left I turned to Bran. "Where did you learn to handle boats?" I enquired.

"I'm from Cornwall, a little fishing village called Mousehole. Near enough got born on a boat and spent most of my younger years in and round them!"

"Can you get the Dory close to the shore, close enough to attract some interest from those beasts?"

He nodded.

"Then can you get us back out fast?" That was the problem with the plan, spend too long getting a specimen and we might be swamped with others and end up in the water. Not a pleasant prospect.

"I think so." He smiled. "It will be just like getting the boat in and out of the sea caves round Mousehole." He didn't pronounce it Mousehole but Mowzel. I guessed it must be some Cornish thing or it might have been the National Speak like a Pirate day?

"Except these sea caves have got teeth and want to eat you." I laughed.

Jay and Beata returned giggling loudly, Beata had an armful of rope of varying sizes and Jay came in beaming with an old lobster pot he'd found amongst a pile of old junk.

"We can use this, push it onto the thing's head and it can't get anywhere near us."

I was gobsmacked, I really didn't think he had it in him, it was just perfect. I sat them down around the table and went through the plan. We'd take the dory, get inshore just before high tide to avoid the beasts walking out at us across the mud en masse and lure one or two into the water. Jay and I would snare a beast with lassos made from the ropes and Beata would smash the lobster pot onto its head, we'd then pull the thing on board and get out of there fast and back to safety and Doc Howard.

I sent Bran to check on the Dory. I was particularly concerned about the fuel situation, I didn't want to get stranded in-shore with a dead engine, and went out onto the pier head. The sun had come up and the temperate was bearable. The decking felt warm, the smell of the salt air was gorgeous, the scudding clouds overhead only heightened my sense of well-being. For the first time in my life, not only did I have a proper girlfriend who wasn't under threat from drug lords or scabrous pimps but a host of other decent people depended on me. Not because they were scared of me, not because they'd tried to rip off Miles but because they respected my judgement and me as a person.

Fion and Steve came out of the cafeteria holding hands, so maybe I'd been wrong about Steve or maybe he swung both ways and both of them smiled at me.

"Everything okay, skipper?" Steve asked.

I nodded back trying to hide my sense of unease. These people actually now saw me as their protector. With power comes responsibility said someone by the name of Ben Parker, Spiderman's uncle, and I was just beginning to realise that that was very, very true.

Tania hailed me; she was sitting in a ghastly green and white deckchair soaking up the sun on the pier head.

"I could come with you." She protested. "You know I can handle myself."

"Not just yourself, nudge, nudge, wink, wink." Again she looked at me as if I was mad, another lost cultural reference.

"No," I said vehemently. "We need to protect all of these people. If Bran and I are away, you are their defender, their guardian. You have to stay."

I could see she was hurt but at the same time she accepted the logic of what I was saying. There were just two people on the pier head who could save the world, and we both knew it wasn't us. We were the star crossed lovers, the ships that passed in the night, the beauty and the beast, the mermaid and the shipwrecked sailor. We had been thrown together for a fleeting moment in a world turned upside down by a parasite that we might be able to destroy, in a world that we could help save.

"Skipper," he yelled, it was catching it seemed. "We seem to have a problem, a big problem." And he pointed upstream.

In the middle distance one of those hideous Thames party boats was bearing down towards us, rudderless and drifting. You know the ones. Cruise on the Thames, drink all night, disco all night and throw up over the side! Carried by the outgoing tide it was moving pretty fast. I could make out zombies in pink party frocks and high heels, zombies in dress jackets and ties, zombies with hipster beards and chinos and zombies in little black dresses, zombies in fishnet tights, zombies who are up all night for good fun, zombies who are up all night to get lucky. The boat was big, far bigger than anything we'd come across, a triple decker with a huge awning at the rear. I wondered how the hell it got through the Thames Barrier but there was significant damage to the hull, it must have collided and bumped its way through like a zombie carrying pinball. It was coming towards us sideways but the trouble was it was a whole lot taller than the pier head. If and when it hit, we were going to have a whole host of the bastards dropping down on top of us. The disco music was still blaring, I could only assume the DJ had an iPod mix and had left it on shuffle. Lazy bastard, I thought and then corrected it, lazy dead bastard.

"All hands on deck," I screamed, and within seconds everyone was on the deck looking at me as if I knew what to do. *Shit, I have to get through this,* I thought.

"Bran, get all the weapons." I yelled and he sprinted off to the RNLI station.

"Steve!" I yelled at him as well. "Go and get every single knife and fork from the kitchens. We are going to need them." And he disappeared back into the cafeteria.

I reckoned we had about two minutes until impact; Bran returned with our arsenal, which to be honest looked a bit puny. I took a Glock and another two grenades, I gave Bran the other Glock, Tania took a shotgun and a box of ammunition, Doctor Howard took another, I looked at her quizzically.

"I was brought up on a farm in Kentucky," she said. "I can shoot as well as anyone."

Fair enough, so I gave her two boxes of shells as well.

Steve returned and distributed the kitchen knives and a whole load of Jamie Oliver BBQ Skewers, other types of skewers are available, about a foot and half long with a hefty metal handle, to the others and we waited, just the ten of us. As far as we were concerned the last remnant of humanity standing together as one on the pier head as a whole shipload of evil bore down on us driven by the tide.

I said to everyone, "Let the people with the weapons deal with them first and if any get through us and on to the deck you have to strike hard and fast. Nothing must be moving on our pier head that isn't human. No messing now, a quick strike directly to the head, nowhere else."

The music changed from "Horny, Horny, Horny" to "Wild Boys" by Duran Duran as the party ship closed on the pier head. I will never forget the sound of the impact and Simon Le Bon's voice on that fateful day as it echoed across the Thames estuary.

I suppose the Argo took the brunt of the impact. As the ship hit the pier deck the Argo crumpled but it did give us just a bit of breathing space and a gap of about six feet between the Thames cruise ship and the pier head. Even so a large number of the beasts were catapulted on to the deck. Tania and Doc Howard were magnificent moving from zombie to zombie and the shotgun blasts reverberated around us like thunder on a sultry summer afternoon. Garish fluorescent dresses and dark dress suits stained in red became the order of the day. Any of them that still moved were dealt with by the infantry with their carving knives and kebab skewers. Doc Clark had pointed out that a skewer through the eyeball seemed to do the trick, thank heavens for her Hippocratic training, and the others quickly learnt from her medical expertise. Bran and I picked off any zombies that appeared on the decks, but it was clear that we needed to do something else to clear the danger as more and more of the beasts appeared on the decks as they realised live prey was present. The Argo continued to crumple and slowly, inch by inch, the cruise ship got closer and closer to the pier head. Bran was shooting at will, good head shots but it seemed there were even more zombies below decks, where the disco area and bar was.

I took another two grenades, I reasoned that the quickest way to the engine room was down the funnel and with a throw worthy of Stuart Broad I launched one and then the other on a parabola. They sailed through the air, one missed by a long way and bounced onto the deck by the door way but exploded tearing apart another group of zombie partygoers but the other hit the mark. Like Luke Skywalker's epic shot at the Empire's Death Star it vanished into the gaping maw and then exploded with a mighty crump. The cruise ship convulsed, Simon Le Bon died in mid verse "Wild boys never lose it, wild boys . . ." and a huge gout of flames exploded from the funnel. It shook the pier head but slowly, ever so slowly the ship, its back broken and wreathed in flame began to settle into the water. The zombies became even more enraged but the weight of the sinking boat meant that it wasn't getting closer to our pier head. As it sank below the level of the deck it became clear that we weren't going to have a problem with any of the beasts getting on to our decking.

"Bran, get the boat hooks!" I yelled above the carnage and in seconds he'd returned with them. "Save your ammunition," I cried. "They can't get to us now." And as the deck sank below the level of the pier deck we could see the zombies milling about on the cruise ship deck below us. The ten of us set about the zombies below and with a boat hook each rained killing blows on them from above. Lusty blow after lusty blow cracking blonde, brunette and grey haired skulls alike, until the party deck sank to the level of the waves and nothing thereafter came out on deck to bother us. Smoke still billowed from the funnel and there were occasional explosions from below decks but the threat had passed.

In shocked silence we all stood there exhausted, terrified but triumphant. I don't know how but once again we'd done it.

Chapter 9: Where Were We? Oh Yes . . . Work to Do

"Guys," I said, "that was awesome, but we still have work to do. Bran get the Dory ready and Beata and Jay let's get ready for the snatch. The rest of you can clear the mess off the decks and get those bodies into the water otherwise the stench will be unbearable."

"Aye, aye Skipper." Bran saluted me in a good natured way. Jay and Beata held hands and followed Bran. We boarded the Dory by the side of the slipway and with everything in place headed for the shore. The sea was still relatively calm, we hadn't had any winter storms yet and we made good progress. I asked Bran to head for a strip of the café's built in arches where a road made its way up the old sea cliffs that made up Southend esplanade. They were known locally as "The Arches" which just proved how little imagination some people had.

The esplanade looked to have a number of zombie walkers and Bran slowed the Dory down about twenty yards offshore. A number of the zombies were now aware of us and made their way onto the small beach area in front of the sea wall. Jay and Beata readied themselves and we banged on the side of the boat and hollered to lure them further out. One in particular looked mighty angry or mighty hungry or perhaps both and made his way through the water towards us. One of his eyes was missing and his clothes hung off him in taters, there were bite marks on his face and shoulders, his death must have been vile, his actual death might just save the world.

Jay got a lasso around him, the noose was good and pinned its arms against its chest, and Beata readied herself with the lobster pot. Jay started hauling the beast towards the boat and then both Bran and I realised there was huge flaw in the plan. We couldn't get the beast on to the boat. Bringing it over the side would destabilise us and we might all end up in the water, there was no room at the stern because of the outboard motor and bringing it over the upswept bow was impossible due to the height and the dead weight involved. Jay was leaning further and further out, straining to pull the beast closer. I shouted a word of warning to Jay and even as the words left my mouth something hit the side of the boat on the opposite side to Jay and the zombie. The boat rocked dangerous and for a minute I thought we'd all end up in the drink. It was too much for Jay, overbalanced as he was, he toppled into the sea. I turned to see what had hit us and came face to face with a ravenous zombie, the skin on its face pockmarked and peeling, now trying to crawl onto the Dory. I smashed its vile rotten fingers with the handle of the Glock, it fell backwards into the sea and I put a shot right through its forehead.

By this time the water on the other side of the boat was foaming red, Jay surfaced for a minute screaming in pain and his eyes pleading with us to help him; he had bites on his face and neck. A host of hands reached for him to drag him back under, Beata screamed.

"Do something for him please."

Bran raised his Glock and as cool as you like put a single shot right between his eyes. Jay disappeared beneath the foaming red water and we never saw him again. Bran turned his attention to the outboard, revved it up and reversed us out of there. Beata was still screaming and crying, I tried to put an arm around her but she screamed something at me in Polish. So I left her on the seat and no one said a word. The journey back was excruciating, we'd lost one of our own and after everything we'd been through together it was heartbreaking.

We docked by the slipway, tied up the Dory and silently went up to and through the doors. The others were all there, looking at us expectantly.

"Jay?" Tania enquired, I shook my head, Beata ran to Tracy, dissolving in tears, Tracy hugged her and they both turned and headed to the café.

"Steve, go and get them something to drink, better give Beata something strong!"

Steve winked at me and went off to help as best he could. Dr Howard looked at me and raised an eyebrow.

"Plan A didn't work," she said. "Is there a Plan B?"

"There's always a way, you just have to find another way of doing things. The plan would have worked . . ."

Then I saw it, the answer. It was so simple it had been staring me in the face from the very first day.

I explained the plan to Bran and he could see that there was some sense in it, I sent him to collect the necessary gear. The others looked aghast as I said, "Okay, we've an hour or so of high water and I want to try again but I still need a volunteer or two. We have to get some live ones for Doctor Howard."

Fion and Doctor Clark stepped forward as one. That was pretty brave of both of them but I could see they both wanted to avenge Jay in some way.

"Thanks you guys, we made some errors last time but this time I think we've a way of getting our prey." They glanced at each other, I really didn't think they knew what we were up against, but they were sure going to find out.

"Doc, when we get it back where do you want it?" That was something else we hadn't really discussed. I didn't want a zombie here for long, tied up and secure it was still a menace if it managed to get free, we'd have wholesale panic on our hands.

"I've had a look round the RNLI station," she responded. "And there's a chart room with a conference table in it. The conference table is big enough to take a body and it's got steel legs that are welded to the floor. We can tie it up in there face down so I can get to the brain stem. It's big enough for me to work in there with the beast and it's secure. Once it's in there I can work with it. I will only come out if the serum is a success or the beast is dead." She smiled. "Either way, I will only come out if it's dead."

"Can't say fairer than that Doc. Bran's here, let's get going." And we trooped back into the slipway area and down to the Dory.

Bran steered the Dory to the same location, he put it into neutral and we banged and hollered just as before. Doc Clark got a rope around one of the more inquisitive and hungrier beasts and then I put plan B into operation. As the Doc pulled it closer I whipped a lifebelt over its head, and then another. The lifebelts were on little stands all over the pier deck "Only to be used in case of Emergency" it read. Well, this *is* a pretty big emergency. The effect of that was instantaneous, its arms were trapped. I snuck another lasso across its shoulders and as Bran reversed away from the beach it floated with us. Fion smacked the lobster pot down on its head as well, and with the zombie raging and baying we made our slow but triumphant way back to the pier head towing behind us a floating, very angry, very inhuman monster, its body ringed by two red and white lifebelts.

This time when we got to the slipway Bran and I got out, along with Doc Clark, who'd already shown her prowess with the oars, we held the two ropes taut with the beast in the middle. It couldn't get to either of us so long as we held it tight. We moved together and got the zombie through the doors and into the conference room without too much trouble. It couldn't bite us because of the lobster pot and it couldn't attack us as it couldn't move its arms.

Together we manhandled it onto the table and slid the lifebelts down below its waist, grabbing each arm and securing it to the welded legs; we slid the lifebelts off completely and secured its legs in exactly the same way. Its head enmeshed in the lobster pot hung over the end of the table. It was snarling and baying but it couldn't do anything about it. The stench from the beast was horrendous though and Dr Howard put vapour rub on her top lip in an attempt to protect her from the worst of the smell. She had brought into the room the bag that she had when we rescued her from the Holiday Inn; she placed it on the side and turned to us.

"You guys can leave me to it, and thank you both, you did a really good job." She beckoned towards the door, Bran left but I decided to stay. Nothing like furthering your knowledge of your enemy I reasoned. It had helped me in my previous life; it might just help me now.

Doc Howard looked at me quizzically, I shrugged back. "I'm here to learn, Doc." I smiled at her.

"The brain stem is the central trunk of the mammalian brain, consisting of the medulla oblongata, pons and midbrain, and continuing downwards to form the spinal cord. . . . I will be testing you later." She laughed. "What I am going to do is get to the spinal cord and see if we can uncover the parasite, if we can then we are going to see if we can kill it using the serums I've perfected. If we do it dies and we win, if we don't it dies and we try again. It's a simple as that."

Then she got to work, using a scalpel she cut into the neck of the zombie, it felt no pain whatsoever, exposing the first few vertebrae of the neck.

"The brain stem controls the flow of messages to all the parts of our body. The parasite is introduced into the body in the saliva as a larva. It then makes its way to the brain stem, matures into a tiny parasite and hacks into the brain stem using neurotoxins it makes for itself, it kills the host and then reanimates it and when it takes over control it instructs the host body to do nothing more than to find other hosts to bite to propagate the species. It's a primal instinct, the survival of your species."

As she spoke she worked carefully with the scalpel, under a magnifying lamp her hands were extraordinarily steady and she probed deeper and deeper into the neck of the zombie. It started getting dark so I put on the lights when suddenly she announced with some triumph in her voice and pointed it out to me through the magnifying glass: "There we are. That's the parasite, that's the bad boy that's caused all the trouble. It looks like they have run some sort of gene manipulation programme based on a tick and our old friend the Jewel Wasp. Now we have to try and see if our serum will kill the little devil."

She went over to the case and opened it to reveal her laptop and a vast array of little vials, she chose one and using a dropper took a sample from the vial.

"Okay, here goes." And without further ado she put one drop on the brain stem and the parasite. "If it works the parasite will die and so will the subject." I stared at the little tick through the glass but what we both wanted to happen didn't, the zombie kept moaning and moving. Dr Howard tutted in disgust and said, "Well that's a failure, I am afraid to say."

She got another of those skewers from the bag and punched it right through the zombie's ear into its inhuman parasite controlled brain. It stopped moving immediately.

She powered up her laptop and started typing.

Subject 1. Brain stem exposed, parasite revealed. Serum A failed.

"How many serums do you have in there," I asked out of curiosity.

"One hundred and twelve," she replied, "and I'll need another subject tomorrow, in fact I need as many as you can get me!"

I sighed; it was turning out to be bloody hard work dealing with this zombie apocalypse. I dragged our friend, Subject 1, off the table, through the lifeboats station and bundled the lifeless body off the slipway and into the cold waters of the estuary. The current tumbled him over and over but he was soon lost to sight. I shivered in the early evening cold. Time for some food and a drink with everyone else, I thought, it's been a funny old day!

Chapter 10: Subjects, Subjects, Subjects

The next day we did six sorties and I took six bodies down the slipway and tumbled them into the Thames and the day after six more, in the meantime our little enclave kept ticking over, the power didn't go off but the food store started to dwindle quite alarmingly. Steve and Fion got on like a house on fire, both had had partners prior to the apocalypse but they worked in the kitchens together and provided a great deal of company to each other. Beata and Tracy did whatever was asked and Tracy in particular kept flicking admiring glances at Bran who seemed oblivious to her obvious charms and the two Doctors worked tirelessly sharing the workload. It can't have been easy for them going into that dank, stinking hellhole day after day with no success. By the end of October, the nights were really drawing in and it was getting a helluva lot colder on our exposed little platform above the sea. On All Hallows' Eve, the 31st of October and subject 53 we hit the jackpot.

Dr Howard came bursting out of the Lifeboat station, her hair dishevelled, shouting and screaming with delight.

"Got it, got it!" she yelled. "We've got it. The parasite is dead and so is the subject."

We were just about to make another snatch off the shore but we didn't have to do that anymore. We whooped and hollered and hugged one another.

"That's great news!" I beamed at Doc Howard, "Well done!"

"I couldn't have done it without all of you guys; you might all have just saved what's left of humanity."

"I've been waiting for this moment." Steve shouted out at the top of his voice, "Special meal for everyone tonight!" and he rushed off to the cafeteria to rustle up our celebratory feast.

Bran looked at me and smiled. "Okay, it's brilliant news but what do we do with this information." A pretty sensible question given that the satellite phones hadn't rung once in well over a fortnight.

"We have to get it to London," said Dr Howard, "there are people there working on the same problem and I need to tell them what we've found so they can begin to mass produce the serum and deliver it to the frontline."

"The frontline?" Tania queried. "We've not seen a plane or a chopper for weeks. Is there really anything left in London?"

"Let's have that meal first and then we'll discuss this tomorrow. We have to do something with this information." I ushered everyone back into the cafeteria away from the biting cold easterly that was sweeping in over the North Sea.

The meal was superb, Steve did us all proud. Using the ingredients to hand we had oxtail soup, out of a tin, the main was pizza, homemade bases and toppings from a variety of tins and for desert, fruit cocktail and dream topping. I didn't even know you could buy dream topping still. We had a few bottles of wine to go with it. Then Bran, Tania and the two Doctors and I sat around a table and started to plan.

Bran started. "I suggest we take the Atlantic 85 lifeboat, there's still plenty of gas in store here, take Doctor Howard and the skipper and we blast up to London do a recce round the MI6 building. If the scientists are there we can deliver the serum and skedaddle it back here. Tania stays to hold the fort; we won't be gone more than two or three days at most."

It seemed a simple plan and for me pretty logical. I looked around the table, I knew Tania wanted to come but Bran was right, we needed someone here who could use a weapon. We were leaving Dr Clark, Tracy, Beata, Fion and Steve here and we had to provide them with armed protection. Tania will have one of the shotguns and one of the Glocks, everyone here has a boathook and there are enough knives to go around. We will take the other weapons, three boathooks and half the grenades, Tim has his axe and Dr Howard has her BBQ skewers.

Dr Howard nodded, and then to my relief so did Tania and Dr Clark. I know what some of you are thinking, ten people and then I'd accepted it, the group being divided up into a seven and a three! To be honest, living with other people had helped my OCD a lot, living with death as a constant companion helped a bit too I suppose, with everything going on it just wasn't that important as when I lived on my own. There you go, every cloud's got a silver lining, a zombie apocalypse can help cure OCD.

"Right," I said, "that's settled." I topped up everyone's glasses and raised my own. "Farewell and adieu to you sweet Spanish ladies, farewell and adieu to you ladies of Spain." I did a pretty mean Quint impersonation. Everyone laughed except Tania, who looked at me with bewilderment; she had a lot of catching up to do with regards to pop culture.

Chapter 11: We Are off to See the Queen . . . Maybe

November 1st dawned with lumpy grey skies and drizzle; it wasn't going to be a great day for farewells. Bran checked the boat early on. Around 9 a.m. we congregated just above the slipway, dressed in full bad weather gear filched from the RNLI stores, big black boots, large waterproofs and orange helmets, heartfelt and teary goodbyes were made, Steve provided us with packed lunches and flasks of hot coffee and the three of us trudged down to boat.

I kissed Tania goodbye. "Look after my motorbike," I joked.

None of us sure what we were going into and dreading leaving behind ones we'd got to like and love. Bran started the engines and sitting astride the seat he engaged the drive and we swept out into the Thames headed for the main shipping lane. On the pier head the little band of survivors watched us go waving until they faded into the grey drizzle. The ride was not pleasant, the boat bounced around in the light chop, it had a solid keel with bright orange inflatable sides, two huge outboards at the stern and a central steering position. The Doc and I sat opposite each other just behind Bran as he wrestled with the wheel. Bran reduced the speed a bit and the ride became more comfortable as we headed up stream passing below the grand old ruins of Hadleigh Castle, made famous by Constable and it was also the site of the 2012 Olympic mountain bike event, you could just make out the torturous track from the boat.

The great oil refinery at the west end of Canvey Island smouldered and burned, dark thick smoke still billowing from the fires and drifting across the river, the acrid smoke was rich in hydrocarbons, and Bran opened her up, we kept our collars up as we sped through it as quickly as we could. Continuing upstream we passed the huge London Gateway container port with its giant cranes, like massive long dead dinosaur skeletons hanging lifeless over the River Thames. Bran throttled back the engines and we took a break with a cup of coffee.

"How far do you reckon we will get today," Doc Howard asked.

"It's hard work going against the tide," said Bran. "I reckon if we get to Rainham Marshes we will need to start thinking of finding somewhere to overnight, much further than that and we will be in heavily populated areas and I really don't fancy our chances of finding anywhere safe." None of us fancied that prospect but we all knew couldn't travel through the night, Bran had been dodging all sorts of debris on our journey so far and if we hit something substantial in the dark that would be the end of our mission.

"As I recall," I said, "there's an RSPB riverside café near the car park, well away from the main road. If the car park is empty it might well be worth taking a look. We can leave the boat tethered securely and maybe find a place of refuge for the night."

We finished the coffee tossed the dregs over the side and Bran set off again. By now the river was narrowing, no longer the vastness of the Thames Estuary, we turned south to follow the meander and then east as we headed for the old port of Tilbury. Up ahead we could see the imposing structure of the Queen Elizabeth Bridge, abandoned cars and trucks littered the carriageway some hanging precariously over the edge. It was eerie going under it and not hearing a single car. We passed abandoned cargo ships, grain stories and warehouses and then reached the isolated Rainham Marshes bird sanctuary. Bran cut the engine and we headed slowly to the shore. He nudged the boat onto the slipway and I leapt on the concrete, rope in hand, and secured the boat to a breakwater. All three of us crawled to the top of the ramp, keeping as low a profile as possible.

The café was fairly new, but there were two cars in the car park. Doc Howard and Bran had large carving knives tucked in their boots, I had my trusty fire axe, we had to be careful about noise, even in a place as desolate and isolated as this. I motioned for Bran to check out the cars and he crawled over and down to the car park. Doc Howard and I moved to check out the café. There was a huge steel fence around it, but the single gate was unlocked, it creaked ominously as opened it and Bran, mouthing "nothing there", joined us as we moved upwards towards the café. It was set on a levee so punters could watch over the wildlife on the numerous ponds and salt marshes. There were half a dozen wooden steps up to the door and as I put my foot on the first one two zombies burst through the double doors and hurtled towards me. I didn't have a chance to raise the axe, in their haste they fell down the steps, knocking me completely off my feet. My helmet was still on otherwise I think they would have knocked me out as my head hit the path with a mighty crack. Bran moved fast and with a swift blow he buried his knife in the neck of the larger beast, Doc Howard with her trademark coup de grace whipped her knife straight into and through the ear of the second, but not before it tried to take a bite out of my helmet.

I stood up, a tad shakily, picked up the axe off the floor and nodded in thanks to them both. Knife in hand I went back up the steps. I opened the café door, waited a second or two and then entered, axe at the ready. It appeared all clear, Bran and I moved stealthily checking everywhere and everything we could, the washrooms, behind the counter, the food stores, even behind the vending machine. Then, taking one of the poles used to guide the queue to the counter I went outside and secured the gate with it. Back in the café, I tied the double doors with good strong rope and then it felt good enough for us to get our waterproofs off and relax a bit. It wasn't that late, about 6 p.m., but it was getting dark, no lights for us tonight. I sprung open the vending machine with the axe and we supplemented our packed lunch sandwiches, with chocolate bars and fizzy drinks. Doc Howard belched uncontrollably on her coke and Bran and I giggled like schoolboys on a weekend camping trip. We agreed to spell three watches and be back on the river by dawn. Bran took first watch and I snuggled into my waterproofs and settled down for the night. Bran woke me around 1 a.m., gently shaking me by the shoulders, his eyes told me we had company and I heard the fence that I had secured shaking. I held my fingers to my lips and we both waited. Whatever it was it gave up, the noise subsided so I mouthed "go to sleep" to Bran and within minutes he was snoring gently.

At 5 a.m. I roused them both, Doc Howard wasn't happy that I hadn't woken her for her watch but I figured it had been a cold and uncomfortable night and she'd needed her sleep. We were all quite happy to be leaving this place, after we used the washroom we were ready to leave, I warned them to be quiet, whatever it was that we heard last night it might still be out there. I undid the rope and we slipped out the door, I had my axe in hand, and down the path, the pole was still in place at the gate, I lifted it and we sneaked through and headed for the slipway.

It came over the slipway hard and fast, snarling at us, red eyed and jaws open, charging towards us at pace, I had my axe out and had time to get a really good low sweep at the thing, I hit its knees cutting both of its legs out from underneath it. It tumbled over and over ending up at Bran's feet, he didn't even bother with a knife just stamped on its head with his heavy boots. The beast's head exploded, Bran looked faintly disgusted, but simply wiped his foot on the zombie's jacket and carried on up the ramp. The boat was as we'd left it. Quickly we pushed it into deeper water, Bran got in and started the engine, Doc Howard took her seat I scrambled over the side and we were off again.

Dawn broke behind us, but there was no warmth from the sun. As we headed towards London, the vast metropolis of 12 million people . . . I wonder how many of them would be zombies, I shivered, with the cold I told myself, not with fear.

Heading east our next destination was the Thames barrier, there were a number of ships and boats wrecked against the inside piers but the two central ones were clear and we sailed through with no major incidents. The sun had risen quite considerably but the persistent low mist still hung around the river refusing to be burnt off by the sun. We motored past London City Airport and the cable car that linked the Excel centre with the vast dome of the O2. Cable cars dangled in the breeze far above us and I swear I saw movement in one of the capsules.

Rounding the great meander loop of the Isle of Dogs, the financial hub of the East End of London, Canary Wharf appeared looming out of the mist and then we swept down to Greenwich and the beautiful Cutty Sark, we then turned northward and eventually got to St Katherine's Dock about midday. Just past the dock we passed under the grandeur of old Tower Bridge and on the right we slipped past the Tower of London in all its glory as it stood sentinel of the north bank.

It was eerily quiet, all you could hear were our outboard motors, not a plane in the sky, not a bus or a car on the streets, just walkers, walking everywhere. Hearing our engine in the distance they rushed to the edge of the embankment and bayed in huge numbers as we made our way past the Globe, the Tate Modern and the London Eye. It was unreal, it was surreal, it was as if every zombie in London was staring at us with those hungry red eyes, sometimes ten or twelve deep. It was very, very unnerving. The malevolent mobs thronged the bridges: London Bridge, Blackfriars, Westminster Bridge and in the distance Vauxhall Bridge and what we hoped would be our final destination.

The green and white edifice that was the famous MI6 building loomed large before us and Bran slowed the boat to a crawl as we drifted closer. There was a slipway to the north of the building but we kept our distance until we could ascertain the situation. The high embankment wall precluded any landing there and I was very unsure of using any slipway with the huge numbers of undead we'd seen on our journey upriver. Bran yelled and pointed as the mob tore around the side of the building, filling the large landscaped garden area between the building and the river. They stumbled through the ornamental ponds crushing each other in the hope of catching our scent or eating our flesh.

This was heartbreaking, all this way for nothing. I looked at Doc Howard who had tears in her eyes, Bran looked totally dejected, what the hell were we to do now?

There were a number of motor cruisers in the middle of the river, moored to a cylindrical floating pontoon, I pointed them to Bran and he nodded and we made our way across the river to them. One in particular caught my eye. It looked brand new, vast cockpit with a sweeping roof, white majestic and very, very desirable. Bran looked at me and I nodded, he tied up astern and we poked our heads over the transom, nothing moved. Cautiously we scrambled into the rear deck area. I beckoned Doc Howard over and she passed me our weapons, three boathooks, our dwindling supplies and her medical bag before joining us.

"Wow," she said, "this is something special."

"It certainly is," Bran said enthusiastically, "it's a Princess 60, one of the best boats money can buy. I used to look at these with envy when they were belting round the Cornish Riviera, cruising between Plymouth and the Scilly isles. As I recall it's got three cabins, each with its own en-suite, it's got a flybridge." I looked at him quizzically. "It's a flying bridge, up above us, there's a second bridge, for better visibility, it's even got its own desalination plant, the whole thing comes in at about one million pounds."

"How much?" Doc Howard and I asked the same question at the same time, completely incredulous.

"It's the best there is." And Bran took us on a tour.

It was astonishing, white soft pile carpets that you sunk into while you walked on, a teak kitchen area as big as the lounge in my flat, three huge bedrooms with superbly appointed bathrooms and a lounge area that was capacious and comfortable. It reminded me of Miles' penthouse in many ways with large white leather armchairs and sofa. On the coffee table was a box of goodies, a bottle of Moët & Chandon champagne, a large case of Peroni, a box of teabags, a jar of coffee, a toilet roll, a bowl of apples and a bunch of flowers. The apples and flowers were desiccated and dead but we all saw the note, attached to the flowers.

I picked it up and read: "Sir, welcome board your new Princess 60, we hope you enjoy this state of the art experience, to complement the experience we've taken the liberty of filling the tank for you and have provided you with this small welcome aboard pack! We hope you enjoy many years of cruising fun."

"Result!" I chuckled, maybe today wasn't turning out all bad. By now dusk had fallen and we were exhausted. We had a few curled up sandwiches, a lot of chocolate bars but also had beer and champagne. We shucked off our outer clothes and settled down in the unbelievable comfort of the lounge. The champagne cork popped, the beer was opened, the sandwiches scoffed and the choccie bars consumed, we were having a wail of a time lounging on the armchairs when I paused in mid mouthful as I heard something that I'd not heard for ages, a phone ringing . . . it was the satellite phone.

Quickly I scrambled among my things and found it in one of the many pockets that the waterproof had, I dragged it out and pressed the answer button.

"Sarah, Sarah Vine is that you? It's Giles where have you been, we've been tracking you by GPS but your movements have been a bit erratic to say the least."

"It's not Sarah but Bran and Doctor Howard are with us. Who am I speaking to please?"

"Doctor Howard is safe and Bran too, that's splendid news. This is Major Giles Griffin of MI6, we sent Sarah and Jason to find Doctor Howard as we thought she was our best bet of dealing with this abomination. Where are Sarah and Jason?"

"They didn't make it I am afraid, it's a long story. Doctor Howard is here and I've put it on speakerphone, you can talk to her if you wish."

"Doctor Howard, how are you. I can't believe that after all this time I am talking to you. The situation is extremely serious. Have you

managed to isolate the cause of this vile disease."

"Yes I have, and I have found a serum that appears to work. It can be easily manufactured and delivered in an airborne way. I believe that this bioterrorism can be countered swiftly and efficiently. Have you the ability to manufacture and deliver the serum in large quantities across the world?"

"Our capability is severely reduced, but there are still pockets of Government operating in and around London and the UK. We are in touch with other Governments around the world just waiting to hear from scientists like you. Where are you now?"

"We are moored by Vauxhall Bridge opposite MI6 HQ, but it seems to have been overrun by the undead."

"It was, I am afraid, just after we sent Sarah and Jason to get you. Those early days were a shambles, complete and utter mess, my men thought they saw a boat coming upriver and I guessed it might be you. We are back at the Tower of London. It's probably one of the most secure parts of London. The walls are still impregnable and the walkways along the river are blocked by old containers, we managed to get them in place before things fell apart. Are you safe for the moment and do you have the serum?"

"We are safe, and yes I do have the serum with me. I am being well cared for, Bran and Tim have been superb. We are in large motor cruiser but we have the original boat as a tender."

"*Brilliant, it's way too late now to be moving safely on the river, stay safe tonight and then tomorrow morning at first light come back down the river, the walkway around the Tower is secure but it's still safer to moor the big boat in the river on a pontoon and bring the tender into the Tower through Traitor's Gate.*"

Doc Howard looked at me. I nodded.

"That's fine by us see you tomorrow morning."

She hung up and put the phone down, today, it seems was turning out just fine.

Then we heard the bump. It came from the bow. I picked up an axe and Bran a boathook. The walkway was wider than most boats but it still required care in the dark. "It sounded like it came from the mooring," I whispered to Bran. It was then I saw it hanging from the mooring rope, it must have fallen in and been carried by the current catching up on our mooring rope, it was barely moving, its leg bashing against the hull. Bran moved towards it swinging the boathook menacingly and whacked it once on the head. The hook sunk in deep, the creature let go of the rope and it sank like a stone, with the boathook still lodged in its skull. Bran tried to wrestle the hook free but he left it a fraction too late and with a muffled oath he stumbled and fell into the dark water with an almighty splash. I dropped the axe and ran frantically to the cockpit, I scrambled onto the transom and leapt into the lifeboat. I had one chance. He was flailing in the water trying to fight against the flow. I held onto the ropes that lined the inflatable and leaned out as far as I could go. Our hands touched, then slipped and then by some miracle I grasped his hand and pulled him alongside spluttering and shaking with the cold and then with an almighty heave back onto the boat. We both lay their gasping.

"Bloody hell," I said, "that was close."

He smiled at me. "Here's to swimming with bow legged woman." The bastard, his Quint impersonation was a whole lot better than mine.

We got back to the cruiser, The White Pearl, as I'd already named her in my mind and he dried off as we worked our way through the remains of the alcoholic picnic.

I woke up the following morning on the huge double bed; weak autumn sunlight was shining through the windows. It was so quiet it was uncanny. I stumbled into the lounge to find Doc Howard already had the kettle on.

"Black coffee . . . er . . . or black tea?" she smiled. "That's all there is."

At that moment Bran joined us, he informed us he'd been up early checking the boat and she was ready to roll. The Princess people had kindly left the keys in the ignition.

"And if they hadn't," I asked, taking a sip of the coffee.

He grinned. "There's always a way."

After we had a meagre breakfast it was time to roll.

Bran took me up to the flybridge and showed me the controls. There was a black leather seat and a steering wheel. It looked much like a car dashboard.

"That's the starter," he indicated. "And then it's just a matter of engaging the gears."

He hit the starter and the engine caught first time. The sound was beautiful, much smoother and quieter than the ugly roar of the two outboards on the lifeboat, it wasn't quite a purr but it did sound delightful.

I made my way forward and cast off the bow line, the current picked us up and we started to move gently. Bran reversed us in to the flow and then as we swung around he put it into forward gear and touched the throttle, the boat surged forward and we turned downstream, heading back towards Tower Bridge.

The ride was so smooth compared to the bone shaking that we'd got in the lifeboat, we slipped between the bridges, and whilst our progress was not totally silent it didn't attract the interest of the undead as much as we had done yesterday. When we got to the Globe Theatre Bran slowed the engines and we glided along, finding a large floating pontoon just after the old battleship HMS Belfast and just before Tower Bridge. Bran judged it perfectly and with a soft touch he stopped us by the pontoon. I made sure the bow line was secure and we all joined up the aft cockpit. We could see the old walls of the Tower of London and the dark shadow that was Traitor's Gate. Grimly, we climbed over the transom and settled down again in the orange lifeboat.

With a flourish Bran started the engines and swept across the river. Slowly we approached Traitors Gate, we went through the first tunnel under the walkway, for a split second emerging into light and then through the darkness of the second tunnel under the great walls before emerging actually inside the Tower of London. There were large steel gates that had been opened for us and now they closed behind us with a hollow clang as they finally shut. There were a few brick steps that led from the water to a low wall and at the top on the wall were a line of soldiers, fully armed with carbines pointed at us.

"Major Griffin is expecting us," I said with as much gravity as I could muster and the line of soldiers parted as a distinguished grey haired man emerged from behind the first rank. He was in uniform but the uniform looked tatty and well worn. He came down the steps confidently towards us. He held out his hand as Doc Howard rose from her seat clutching her bag and helped her from the boat escorting her up the steps. He turned to look at Bran and I as if we were idiots.

"Come on, you two," he said, "no time to lose."

We followed as the line of soldiers dispersed but two of them accompanied us as we trailed behind the Major and the Doctor. I remembered from a school visit that there were two walls and the central keep, the White Tower. It looked like we were headed for the White Tower. As we crossed the open area we both noticed lots of soldiers, some slumped down or leaning against walls. Some of them were smoking, some were eating and some were just asleep.

"How long have you guys been here?" I asked our companions.

"Since it all kicked off," the younger one said. "We were mobilised and came in to the City from Surrey but we lost half the regiment in the first few hours. Luckily we were able to get back here, and ever since then we've been pinned down. The defences are pretty strong, but every day it gets harder. The men are exhausted."

Bran and I exchanged glances, I wasn't sure that this was exactly what I'd expected. We reached the White Tower and went up the wooden steps, keeping the Major and the Doc in sight.

We reached a room and were ushered inside, the room wasn't vast but of a good size and there was a rectangular table in the middle of it with about a dozen or so people sat around. No one stood up, but there was an urn in the corner bubbling away merrily and a soldier came over to offer us tea and coffee.

There were three seats for us a long one side and after we'd got our refreshments (with milk) we sat down. Doc Howard in the middle and Bran and I on either side, a bit like her honour guard, which I suppose we were.

Major Griffin took his seat at the head of the table.

"Ladies and gentlemen, this is could be our last hope and it may well be the last hope for humanity. May I introduce to you Doctor Howard and her two companions, er . . ." He'd obviously forgotten us so he carried on, "Doctor Howard has found what may well be the answer to our prayers, a serum that can be delivered by air and we may at last be able to fight back against the hordes outside."

The buzz around the table was palpable; people sat up straighter and began to listen more intently.

"Doctor Howard, this is the cabinet of the United Kingdom, this is one of a handful of military bases left in London. There are a few in the rest of the country and some of them are doing better than we are, but we are in serious trouble. Unless we can mass produce this serum in large quantities very soon then we may lose our grip on the country altogether."

At that point he sat down and everyone started asking questions. They wanted to know about Sarah and Jason so I told them what they wanted to know and then Doctor Howard relayed everything that had happened to her since the Holiday Inn. To be honest I stopped listening at some point, I might even have dozed off. I was startled awake by the sound of gunfire, I jumped to my feet but everyone in the room just carried on talking.

"Don't worry," said the man to my right, "this happens all the time, the bastards never give up trying."

"Tell me about, tell me about it," I said. "By the way, who the hell are you?" His face looked kind of familiar but I wasn't sure.

"Oh, I am the Prime Minister," and he went back to asking questions of Doc Howard.

In the end it was agreed that the Doctor would start manufacturing the serum in the Tower and send the details of it to the various safe havens in the UK and abroad. Some of the materials they had within the walls of the Tower but some would have to be flown in from research facilities up and down the land. It looked like our work was done and just before the meeting broke up I collared the PM once again. I tapped him on the shoulder.

"Look," I said, "we've played our part, it's down to the boffins and the military now. We've got people on the pier deck at Southend we need to get back to them but we need supplies and fresh weapons."

The PM beckoned Major Griffin over and they had a brief discussion. The Major nodded and glanced at the soldier in charge of the refreshments.

"Take these two down to the stores and let them have all the food and weapons that they need, the one thing we are not short of are supplies." He said to me, "When you've got your people you are welcome here, the problem outside will soon be sorted out." He nodded at the squaddie who saluted and about faced.

I thanked the Major and shook his hand. Though I wasn't sure I shared his confidence. We were just about to leave when the PM rapped his knuckles on the table.

"From what I hear," he said solemnly, "Doctor Howard and the serum would not be here without the considerable bravery and courage of these two young men and the rest of the people on Southend Pier. It is within my power to reward courage but there is also someone here who can do that was well. Prince Harry, will you do the honours."

A well-built ginger haired fellow at the end of the table opposite where Major Griffin had been sitting stood up and slowly made his way over to us. I didn't know where to look and I could feel my pulse racing and my cheeks flushing.

"Gentlemen," he said in that wonderful clear tone of his, "as the last surviving member of the Royal Family, I recognise the enormous courage and bravery you have shown in the face of overwhelming odds. You have given us a chance where we thought all hope had vanished. It is part of the indomitable British spirit that the few never ever surrender and you are living examples of that spirit. We are extremely grateful and I would like to reward you for your courage. In the absence of a coronation I am but a simple Prince, but now I am going to be the King very soon and you two have made it possible. As future King it is in my power to knight you both. I do so, and thank you once again." Then he simply shook both our hands.

The room erupted with applause, we mumbled our thanks and stumbled out into the corridor as the enormity of what we had achieved hit home.

"Bloody hell," I said, "wait till Tania hears about this."

The stores were in the basement, a huge vaulted area that probably dated back to the Norman Conquest laden with dried goods, weapons and ammunition. We loaded what we could onto a sack barrow, got more ammunition for the Glock and the shotgun and a couple of cases of grenades and then just as were about to leave I spied a stack of Rocket Propelled Grenade Launchers in the corner.

"We'll take a couple of those if we may," I said. I remembered the issue we had with that bloody party cruise ship, if another came towards us, those little babies would solve the problem long before it became a danger to the pier head. With the sack barrow and the heavy bags slung over our shoulders we made our way back to Traitor's gate and our lifeboat tender. The soldiers opened the gate and we wished each other all the best as we edged back out into the river and across to our cruiser.

It took us a bit of time to get the supplies on board but at last we did and with the lifeboat secure behind us we headed back to Southend. We stopped overnight in the river tied up to a buoy off Gravesend. Even though were both impatient to get back to the Pier Head travelling at night wasn't sensible at all so we agreed on another overnight stop.

Chapter 12: Back Home to a Hero's Welcome, Perhaps.

Once again I woke up in a comfy bed, I really could get used to this life, I thought to myself. I washed and joined Bran for breakfast. Just flakes with honey and some more back coffee and then we got back onto the river. As we got to Old Leigh with its quaint cockle sheds and smart little pubs down by the river you could see the long grey line of the pier ahead. I gasped in horror, as I could also see dark smoke rising from the pier head. Bran saw it at the same time as me and from the fly bridge he pushed the boat to her maximum.

We fairly shot across the water as we sped towards the smoke. A snaking wake of white water plumed behind us as we closed on the pier head. I called to Bran to slow down, we didn't know what was happening and I didn't want us closing too fast. We couldn't see anyone and Bran brought the cruiser to one of the mooring points alongside the wreck of the party cruise ship. I tied us up bow and stern and taking our pistols we crept up the ladder to the pier deck. Poking my head above the ladder I was shocked to find the café a smouldering ruin and the lifeboat station windows and doors all smashed in.

We both crawled across the decking, and then I saw the body at the foot of the steps leading up to the café. It was Steve, we ran over to him and Bran kneeling down covered me as I leant over. Steve was lying on his stomach, I turned him over, his head was covered in blood and then to my astonishment he opened his eyes.

"Steve, what happened?"

"Tim," he murmured, barely conscious. "It's you; I knew you would come back."

Bran ran to the cafeteria and even though the fire had reduced it to a ruin came back with a bottle of water. I opened it and Steve drank thirstily.

"Steady," I said "Not too much in one go. Where are you hurt?"

"They shot me in the head, one of them took a shot at me and I went down. The pain was excruciating." I looked at his forehead and you see the crease mark of the bullet, it had struck him a glancing blow, enough to have drawn copious amounts of blood, enough to have knocked him out but obviously not a killing blow. The blood flow and his inaction, and the fact that he'd fallen onto his stomach had saved his life.

"Okay mate," Bran said, "let's get you over to our prize and get you sorted."

We had medical supplies on board and we'd taken a lot from the RNLI station, just as well as it looked as if it had been looted by whoever was responsible.

Gingerly, we got Steve on his feet and between us guided him down the steps to the cruiser.

"Wow," he said looking around him in awe at the luxurious surroundings, then he gasped and passed out with the exertion.

Later, much later he woke up; we'd cleaned the wound, dosed him up with some antibiotics and fed him a load of co-codamol to take the pain away. He sat on one of the stateroom chairs with a bandage the size of a turban around his head and began telling the story.

"They came for us yesterday morning from the East at sunrise, so we couldn't see what we were dealing with; the sun was really low in the sky and perfect cover as they zig-zagged towards us. On jet skis, there were five of them; they came in fast and hard. We didn't really have time to react before they were on the slipway and on the decking.

"Tania went outside the cafeteria with the shotgun but by that time they'd already grabbed Fion and Beata as they weren't armed and threatened Tania that if she didn't hand over her weapons they'd shoot them there and then.

"Dr Howard and Tracy were still in the cafeteria with me. Tania knew their leader, she called him Jason, he was angry very angry and he only had four fingers on one hand. I noticed that straight away. He kept asking where you were, but no one would tell him. Tania asked him how he got away and he just said, 'There's more out there than you know of, places to live, places to breed, free of zombies, free of everyone, where men can do as they please.'

"'Jason you talk a load of shit,' said Tania and he got really mad.

"'If that's the way you want it,' and he cocked his gun and held it to Doc Howard's temple. That's when Tania put the shotgun down.

"'You in the café,' he shouted. 'Out. You come out now.' And the three of us left the cafeteria.

"'That's it boys,' he said to the others, 'take your girl and it's back to Radio City, tell the supply boat there's rich pickings here.'

"Doctor Howard told them she was a doctor and asked if she could get her medical bag, he nodded so she went back inside to collect it.

"They each took one girl and headed back down to their jet skis, that left him and Tania on the decking.

"'What about me?' I asked.

"'What about you? Fat boy?' He looked at me and as cool as you like and shot me where I stood. I saw his evil grinning face and that's the last thing I remember until you picked me up off the deck."

"That bastard, that fucking bastard, he's going to get fixed, well and truly fixed!" I screamed in anguish and fury. "Not only has he taken all the girls, he's ransacked our stores as well."

"Who is he?" Bran asked, calmly. "And more importantly, where is he?"

I stopped ranting, the only hope we had of getting the girls back was to move quickly and efficiently. Move fast strike fast and act decisively. I took Bran up to the RNLI map room and observation deck. The map was spread out on the chart table.

"Bloody jet skis, what's the range of one of those pieces of shit." I thumped the table in desperation.

"They can't go that far and don't forget on the return journey they had a double load, they left before dusk so they wouldn't risk travelling that far at night, let's look at a 20-mile radius and see what that looks like." Bran got a large pair of nautical compasses and measured a 20-mile radius and scribed it with a pencil on the chart beneath us.

"That's a bloody big area, but," I reasoned, "they must have a dry and secure base to go back to so we are looking for a Radio City, what the hell does that mean? Hang on its coming back to me there was pirate radio station on a fort somewhere in the Thames Estuary in the 1960s, my dad told me about it. It might have been owned by Screaming Lord Sutch at some point."

"There it is!" Bran pointed with delight. "Shivering Sands Army Fort about 15 miles due east from the Pier Head. I'd bet anything that's where those bastards came from. They're probably desperate for stores, so they thought a quick raid on us would tide them over for the winter. But why was this bloke Jason asking after you? That sounded personal."

I told Bran the whole story, the only thing about the whole sorry tale was that I hadn't put a bullet through his mean and miserable skull before I pushed him over.

"That means he must have drifted 15 miles and got to the fort under his own steam." He mused.

"Or somebody found him and in the water and took him there," I added. "Either way; he survived, and he's mighty pissed at me. It really doesn't matter though we just have to get there, we have to take them out and get the girls back, so let's move."

"How many of them are you do you reckon?" Bran asked.

"There's at least five plus the supply boat bloke. There may well be more though. The only difference to what we've faced up until now is that these bastards don't bite, they've just got guns." I grinned.

We hightailed it back to the cruiser. Bran fired up the engine and off we went. I broke out the armoury. The RPG Launchers were unpacked and loaded and extra ammunition in boxes placed to hand, the shotguns were laid about the cockpit with boxes of shells beside them; both Bran and I had the Glocks with full magazines and the box of grenades was stored where it could be got at easily.

The adrenalin was pumping, the wind was blowing, the gulls were calling and we were on our way.

Chapter 13: Radio City

Radio City came into sight at about 2 p.m.; we'd hammered it from Southend Pier the boat smashing over and into the waves in the choppier waters of the North Sea. Radio City consisted of five towers connected by walkways; it was built in 1943, on land and then floated out to sea and sunk onto the sea bed. Each tower consists of an accommodation block fixed on top of four splayed legs. You could almost imagine them as Martian fighting machines from *The War of the Worlds*. I was pretty sure that most of the walkways had collapsed long ago so it was likely that the captives would all be in one place.

Sure enough, as we got closer the individual towers became more defined. One in particular had smoke rising from a chimney and on closer inspection a host of jet skis tied up underneath it on a floating jetty connected to the leg.

By this time our approach had been noticed and a number of people were scurrying around getting the jet skis ready.

"Incoming!" I yelled and prepared myself with an RPG Launcher at the bow. Steve was in the aft cockpit with another RPG launcher. "Here they come."

Soon the air began to fizz and hum with the sound of bullets as the jet skis whizzed about trying to take us out, but we kept on going. The bucking of the little jet skis made it hard for them to aim at anything but we had the benefit of a much more stable platform. I put the RPG launcher on my shoulder and sited it on the nearest one, I pressed the trigger and to my delight it hit it amidships. I whooped with delight as it exploded, and catapulting over the water, the driver landed with a splash twenty yards away.

I heard another crump and Steve whooping with joy as another one bit the metaphorical dust. Before I had time to reload one darted towards the bow and drew alongside with one of our grenades in hand, I grabbed the Glock and caught the driver with a shot before he could launch his lethal cargo. It hit him on the shoulder but it was enough for him to lose control, the boat swerved violently tipping him out into the sea, the grenade exploded very close and he screamed as the foam turned red with gore.

Bran joined in at the point with a great shot, whether by luck or by judgement we'll never know, he hit the petrol tank of another jet ski, the result was astounding. The jet ski exploded in a fireball and another of the drivers found himself on the long journey to Davy Jones' locker. This was too much to bear for the final jet ski he just turned and fled, we chased him back to the pontoon, where he didn't even bother to tie up his craft he just jumped off it and headed for the ladder. I had the shotgun up in a second and as the range shortened I got him before he'd gone even half way up. He fell into the sea another bloody splash was all we saw.

Bran brought the boat to a halt. So far so good, but the worst was yet to come. We'd taken out five of them but who knew how many there were. We looked up to where the ladder disappeared into the tower. The door was shut, what a surprise. I shouldered the RGP launcher again and fired. The way was now clear.

"Steve, stay here," I commanded. "Anyone that isn't one of us, coming down that ladder, shoot 'em."

He nodded grimly, he was obviously in pain, but I knew we could trust him with our lives. We moored the cruiser, we both grabbed our guns and began the climb up the ladder, Bran was covering me with his Glock, it was a nerve wracking climb as I was at my most vulnerable from anything above me, but I made it to the top without trouble, I knelt at the top of the ladder and beckoned Bran up. He scrambled up in double quick time.

At that point a disembodied voice called from above.

"Tim, tiny Tim, where are you," Jason mocked me from above.

Bran tapped me on my shoulder and indicated down the dimly lit corridor, beyond a series of closed doors in the gloom I could just make out a figure tied to a chair with duct tape around her mouth. I recognised her hair first and then the clothes she'd been wearing when Bran and I left. I started to run to her, Bran followed me. I suppose I should have noticed the panic in her eyes, the way she was frantically shaking head but love is blind, so

Chaucer once said, as did Paul McCartney as I recall.

The trap was perfect, a line of monofilament fishing line at ankle height completely invisible in the gloom of the corridor. I hit it hard, and the wedges they were attached to were yanked from two doors. Eight ravenous zombies in tattered clothes tumbled out of the two rooms. I was just ahead of Bran so they missed me completely but they hit him hard. He went down cracking his head on the metal floor with an awful crack. In seconds two of them were making a meal of his neck and face and another tucking into his hand. I shot three of the five remaining who were coming towards Tania and me with the Glock and then the bloody thing jammed. The other two seemed intent on making us their supper. I split one of their heads open with the butt of the Glock and kicked the knee of the other so hard they might have heard the crack in Canvey. It went down and I stamped as hard as I could on its head, neither of them moved after that. By this time the feasting three were beginning to realise that there was more prey. I could just see Bran's Glock lying a few feet away. I ran towards it and like a cricketer saving a four slid to it on one knee picked it and fired in one movement. Three shots, three kills.

Bran was lying motionless, either unconscious or dead, it was with a very heavy heart and a tear in my eye I placed the Glock to his temple and pulled the trigger. If the positions had been reversed I would have wanted him to do the same for me. The Glock clicked on an empty chamber, no ammunition left in this one, I realised with horror.

I recovered my Glock but as hard as I tried I couldn't clear the blockage, moving over to Tania I quickly untied her from the chair. When I pulled the duct tape off she raised her fingers to her lips and indicated upstairs. The stairs were dimly lit but I knew that somewhere up there was my appointment with death. With no weapons I realised that we really were up against it. She pulled my arm and led me back down the corridor.

"We've got no weapons and no hope," I whispered in despair.

"I have an idea," she whispered, and explained it to me, it sounded mad, but mad plans do work, we both had direct experience of this. So she looked me in the eye, I nodded and then she bit my jaw as hard as she could.

Chapter 14: Unlucky for Some

With the blood dripping down my face I made way over to and up the stairs. Slowly I climbed, the only sound the odd splat as a drop of blood hit the risers. At the top of the stairway was a small landing with a door, I opened the door and fell into the room. The room was an observation room of some sort with windows to all sides, the light was fading but the view was still remarkable. On chairs in front of me and hog tied in much the same way as Tania were Doc Clark, Tracy, Beata and Fion. They looked petrified. I groaned and rose to my knees to see Jason in the corner with a huge grin on his face. I moved towards him but he motioned me to stay still, and with one of our Glocks in his hand I wasn't going to argue.

"So, it's little Tim," he sniggered. "I see my friends downstairs made you all welcome. They were stupid idiots who got bitten when I sent them on missions. They have a use though as guard dogs, as you will old sport when you transform into one of them."

I staggered and hit Doc Clark's chair knocking her and the chair to the floor. Her medical bag I kicked in fury and bellowed at him.

"You bastard, you utter bastard, Tania and Bran are both dead! As for me." I indicated the bite. "I am done for, so what's your plan now? What are you going to do with this pathetic sea fortress of yours?" I pointed towards the window where you could see the other parts of the fort, one or two of them still linked by walkways.

"This is going to be my little kingdom," he gloated, "and these fair maidens will be my brood queens. The situation on land is lost as you well know, so I am going to recreate Jerusalem at sea. I am going to re-populate the Earth from this sea fort and spread my genes round the world. Once the population here has reached twenty or thirty I am going to move to one of the old oil rigs in the North Sea taking my subjects with me." He cackled insanely. "It's a shame your little Croatian is dead, I was going to save her till last but I am going to rape them all in front of you. I may start with this chubby little Essex MILF." He squeezed the large fleshy breasts of Fion in a malicious way. "Then move on to these little beauties." He nodded towards Beata and Tracy, "And finish off with the good Doctor. I've always fancied the medical type."

"What a four fingered gutless coward, you are, sub-human and quite pathetic," I spat out the words with as much contempt as I could muster.

Once again I staggered towards him, he panicked a bit as he thought I might try to bite him but his ego was so momentous that he wanted to share his plans for world domination with me in revenge he had no intention of shooting me yet until I'd suffered too.

Out of the corner of my eye I noticed a pale arm reach in from the door and grab the medical bag I had kicked closer to the door. I roared in fury as another distraction and made my way to a set of windows opposite the door. Jason's eyes followed me filled with hatred and malice.

"You are completely insane," I shouted. "You haven't got a hope in hell."

With his back to the door he didn't see Tania run in, he didn't see Tania with the flare gun, that she had retrieved from Doc Clark's medical bag, he didn't see Tania hold it an inch from his back, he didn't see Tania pull the trigger, but he did feel the flare enter his back and ignite in his rib cage. The look of, firstly, astonishment and then total terror was overwhelming. His body glowed, you could actually see his bones through his chest then without warning actual flames erupted from his mouth and his eyeballs. I guess he was dead within a nanosecond but his body remained upright as the flames devoured him from within. Eventually he collapsed smouldering and spitting on the floor.

Quickly Tania and I untied our friends and explained how I actually got the bite. We all went back down stairs where more than a few tears were shed by the side of Bran's body.

After they left and had begun clambering down the ladder to our boat I used Jason's Glock to ensure poor Bran didn't rise again. Within ten minutes we were all back on board the White Pearl. The girls sprawled out on the large leather armchairs talking quietly among themselves. None of them had been seriously injured but they had had to endure Jason's continual groping and lewd suggestions.

Steve busied himself in the galley making hot drinks for everyone and I fired up the engines and set course for Southend Pier. I reckoned we could moor up there for a bit and find out what was happening in London. Tania joined me on the fly bridge, the sun was setting in the distance over Pitsea tip and I put my arm around her waist.

Doc Clark had dressed the bite marks on my jaw, but to be honest I looked a bit like Frankenstein's monster but Tania looked up at me wistfully. I kissed her on the lips, just two star-crossed lovers who'd managed to overcome titanic forces of darkness and evil.

"Did I tell you I am now a Peer of the Realm?" I said.

She looked at me as if I was mad. "You are a pier?" she said incredulously.

(To be continued . . .)

Made in the USA
Charleston, SC
12 October 2016